The Age of Malaise

The Age of Malaise

by Dacia Maraini

Translated from the Italian
by Frances Frenaye

GROVE PRESS, INC.   NEW YORK

The Age of Malaise

1

Cesare's father, wearing his gray flannel, red-lined lounging jacket, opened the door. He nodded his grizzled head by way of greeting, shot me the usual smile and stepped back with a malicious air.

"Looking for Cesare?"

"Yes."

"Let me call him."

Cesare had heard me coming and shouted out to send me straight to his room.

"He's studying," said his father, with a wink. "Exams are coming up next month."

He took me to his son's room and paused, with his hand on the knob.

"Such a good boy!" he exclaimed. "You ought to see the way he works." He could not seem to make up his mind to open the door.

"Well, I'm going to take a look at the paper," he concluded with a timid smile. "Papers, radio and every now and then a cup of coffee, they're all my fun."

Finally he turned the doorknob and let me in. He closed the door quietly behind me, and I could hear him shuffle down the hall in his slippers.

"I've been expecting you for half an hour," said Cesare.

"I was busy."

"Doing what?"

I shrugged my shoulders. Cesare scowled, looking at his long, trim, well-padded fingers.

"Sit down and wait till I've finished the chapter."

The room was cluttered with furniture. The blinds were drawn and there was a stale odor of dust and smoke in the air. Cesare sat in his dressing gown with his elbows propped up on a desk. Books were stacked all around him. The light shone on his blond hair, which grew low at the back of his neck, while a single lock fell across his forehead. He pushed the lock back with one hand and stared attentively at his book.

"No use," he said after a minute, shoving the book away. The dressing gown opened over his smooth, hairless chest.

"How about it?" he asked in an entirely different tone of voice.

"Yes."

"Why didn't you get here earlier? I can't seem to study when I'm waiting for you."

"Because of helping my father with his insurance business."

"I don't believe you."

I peeled off my coat and scarf.

"When you come to see me you really ought to put on something better. I don't like to see you always in the same dirty sweater."

"You'd like to see me in my blue dress, is that what you mean?"

"That or some other. You look like something the cat dragged in. Just look at yourself!"

He got up and pointed to the mirror on the inside of the open door of the wardrobe. I saw the rumpled neck of the sweater and the places where perspiration had made the color run under my arms. I lowered my head.

"Get the idea?" he insisted.

I nodded.

"Don't tell me your father hasn't the money to buy you a new sweater. A cheap one, I mean."

"Where does my father come in? My father's wrapped up in the insurance business. He hardly knows he has a family. But I'm clean underneath. I wash my own underclothes."

"That reminds me . . . get your clothes off."

He closed the wardrobe door and bent his big blond head toward mine. His eyes were blue, gray and yellow, like those of a cat, and his teeth were wide and short. We got undressed and slipped in between the sheets.

"I forgot to lock the door," he grumbled, raising himself up on one elbow.

"Shall I lock it? There's no danger of your father's barging in."

"You never can tell. Sometimes I think he's peeking through the keyhole, like a little boy."

"Why would he do a thing like that?"

"Out of curiosity. Or just for fun."

I felt his cold feet against my ankles. He held me so tight I nearly suffocated. It was quickly over, and he rolled onto his other side to go to sleep. I stared up at the semblance of an embroidery pattern on the ceiling. There were pink, purple and black designs, flowers outspread like trays and leaves as shiny and erect as sword blades. I counted the petals of one flower; there were twelve of them, as I knew perfectly well, although I counted them over uncertainly every time. Under my arm I felt the rhythmical rise and fall of Cesare's shoulder. On the walls there were photographs taken in Holland: a windmill, a canal, broad green meadows, sailboats and barges loaded with flowers tossing on a stormy gray sea. A telephone rang on the bedside table, and Cesare stretched out his hand for the receiver.

"What is it?"

[9]

Then he softened his voice and began talking as if he were alone in the room. His fiancée was calling.

"Yes, I was studying. This evening I've got a stack of work. Five o'clock tomorrow afternoon, what do you say? . . . You know I love you. . . . Here's a kiss. . . . Now you kiss me."

As he hung up he gave a sheepish smile.

"Do you mind?"

"No."

"What nonsense, this getting married," he mumbled, pulling me toward him.

"Why do you go through with it?"

"Don't ask me. I don't know."

"What's the date."

"In April. We'll have to call it quits, you and I."

"You've told me that before."

"What if I still want you?"

"I really don't know what I can do about that."

"Oh well, I'll be too busy. I want to get my degree next year and then a job. Otherwise people will say I married for money."

He got out of bed and into his dressing gown, rolling up the sleeves over his blue-veined white arms. Then he tapped his throat and said it was hurting.

"Too many cigarettes. But how can I study without smoking?"

He lit a cigarette and held it out to me.

"Have one?"

I shook my head. He inhaled deeply and blew the smoke deliberately out of his mouth and nostrils.

"Better get your clothes on. I'll be able to concentrate on my work now, and that's what I've got to do."

He stuck his head out the door.

"My father's nowhere in sight. Maybe he's gone out. I'm going to the kitchen to make some coffee. There'll be a cup for you, too." And he walked down the hall. I followed after.

[10]

His father was sitting beside the kitchen window. His eyes were on the paper, but he seemed to be asleep. He smiled at us and went back to his reading.

"A whole catch of fish contaminated by radiation, isn't that crazy?" he exclaimed suddenly, raising his head.

"Some coffee, Father?"

"Just a little . . . *The fish which was unloaded on the dock at Genoa yesterday morning . . .*" he read. "We might all be poisoned. . . . Yes, just a little more sugar. Good boy, Cesare! You make better coffee than I do."

As soon as Cesare had emptied his cup he impelled me toward the front door, paying no attention to his father, who was still reading the news out loud.

"Good-bye, you sweet thing," his father called after me.

"Hasn't your old man caught on?" I asked Cesare.

"He just pretends he hasn't. He doesn't give a hoot as long as it doesn't give him any trouble."

"Discreet, I call him."

"Nonsense!"

He shut the door behind me, and I went down the stairs, thinking of the way his body got all hot and nervous when we made love and of the brusque, half-angry, half-embarrassed way he handled it.

My father wasn't home when I got there. Soon my mother came in, tired and ill-humored; she went straight to her room with the intention of getting undressed and throwing herself onto her bed.

"Did he say anything today?" she called out anxiously through the open door.

"No."

"You must play your cards close to the chest. Make yourself desirable, and then not give him an inch. Do you understand?"

"Yes."

I could imagine her getting undressed in the cold, bare little room, lit by a lamp without a shade. All the time she was speaking to me in a loud voice about Cesare.

"What did you say, Mother?"

"They must be well off, those people. You've never told me about their apartment. How many rooms do they have?"

"I don't know."

I didn't want to see her, as she unfastened her brassière and looked for her wrapper. The sight of her reminded me that one day I'd be the same way, fat and flabby and wrinkled.

"That's what you always say. You ought to have more respect for your mother. I'm forty years older than you are, and don't you forget it. I've had time to learn what's what, and you'd do well to take my advice. Do you understand?"

She didn't really expect me to answer. As she talked she examined her complexion in the mirror. Lowering her head she singled out a strand of hair and ran it through her fingers to see if the dye was still holding. Then she went and sat on the bed, massaging her feet and mumbling to herself.

"Have you done your homework?" she asked, after several minutes had passed.

"No."

"I'd like to know how you expect to get your diploma if you never open a book."

I did not reply. She went to fetch my books and opened them up on the table.

"Get to work," she said, pushing me toward the chair.

2

I left the house, pulling my undersized coat around me. Water was seeping in through a hole in the sole of one of my shoes. A shiver of cold went up my spine, and I tightened the scarf around my neck. The rain had emptied the streets, and although now it had stopped coming down, they were still deserted. The rain water had collected in the gutters and was running down through the corner gratings. I kept my eyes on the ground so as not to step with my holey shoe in a puddle. I went into a stationery shop and bought a stenographic pad. The shopowner, a thin little man who looked like my father, gave me a kindly smile as he counted out the change.

"Good luck with your work!" he called out gaily.

After leaving the shop I walked along the trolley track in the direction of the Viale XXI Aprile. At a certain point I paused and then crossed the street to make a phone call from the Mocambo Bar across the way.

"Cesare isn't here," said his father's warm voice, "but I'd be glad to give him a message when he comes in."

"No thanks. When do you expect him?"

"My child, I really don't know. He's probably gone to a friend's house to study."

He's gone to see his fiancée, I said to myself as I hung up.

[13]

When I came out it was raining again. I put the scarf over my head and walked close to the wall. I heard the tram just behind and a minute later it stopped a few feet ahead. No sooner had I put my foot on the step than it started jerkily away. As I was pushing my way through the crowd I felt someone jog my elbow.

"Hi, Enrica."

"Hi." He was a boy in my class at school.

"What are you up to?" he asked.

"Nothing special."

He laughed.

"I'm going somewhere to dance," he said. "Why don't you come along?"

"Where are you going?"

"To a friend's house. Giordani. Do you know him?"

I shook my head.

"The tall fellow with the glasses. He's in the class just above ours."

"Oh yes. Where does he live?"

"In the Via Marsala."

"Near school?"

"Just two houses the other side."

The tram was filled with the smell of wet raincoats, and water was dripping from umbrellas onto our feet. I looked at my companion, vainly trying to remember his name. He had an angular face, protruding cheekbones and thin lips.

"How old are you?" I asked him.

"Twenty. What about yourself?"

"Seventeen."

"So are you coming along?"

"All right."

When we got off he grabbed my hand and started running through the rain. My legs and coat were splashed with mud and wet hair was glued to my forehead.

"Some downpour!" he shouted.

We went by the shoe store, where I always stopped as I came out of school to look at the display in the window. Behind the glass the shoes had a special fascination. Now, too, I could not resist staring at them, but my companion tugged at my arm and we went on running toward the end of the street. Finally we stopped in a dark, sheltered entranceway, which stank of cat's urine.

"Tired?" he asked.

"A little bit."

He squeezed my hand, but I pulled it away and began pushing back my hair. My scarf was a rag, and my feet were soaked.

"What a mess!" he exclaimed, looking down at the cuffs of his trousers, which had changed color.

The stairway had high steps and was unlighted. We were out of breath when we reached the top floor.

"What's your name, anyway?" I asked as we waited in front of the closed door.

"Carlo."

Giordani came to let us in. He was wearing a dark suit and his short-sighted blue eyes were open very wide behind his thick glasses.

"Hi."

"Hi."

"Some mess outside!"

The entrance hall was narrow and damp, with framed photographs hanging on the walls. *"To Colonel Giordani from General Giossi,"* I read aloud. Carlo scrutinized the yellowed picture in the heavy gold frame. " *'To Colonel Giordani . . .'* that's all right," he observed pedantically, "but you can't possibly say who it's from because the signature's illegible."

We tagged along after Giordani into the living room, which was large and irregularly shaped, with a heavy glass and wrought-iron lamp hanging from the center of the ceiling.

[15]

A lot of girls were sitting huddled together on a couch, with some boys standing in front of them, nervously puffing at cigarettes.

"Lemonade? No, Pernod!" said Giordani, holding the glass and the bottle up close to his short-sighted eyes and pouring the sticky white liquid.

Beside the phonograph, which was set up in a piece of antique marquetry furniture, there was a whole stack of "45" French and American records, which Carlo now began to look through. The music coming from the loud-speaker was loud and aggressive one moment, faint and sugary the next. Carlo kept time by tapping his heel on the floor.

"What's Giordani's first name?"

"I don't remember." And he added, puckering his lips and with a note of satisfaction in his voice: "His father retired from the army after fighting a whole bunch of wars and getting all sorts of hardware pinned on him."

Giordani was making the rounds, bottle in hand. Every time someone held up a glass to be filled he put in a plea for dancing.

"Are you sure you're having a good time?" he asked awkwardly. "Why don't you get out there on the floor and dance?"

But nobody moved. Finally he himself pulled one of the girls to her feet and whirled her around the room.

"It's rock 'n' roll," he said at the end of the record, wiping the perspiration off his forehead. "I don't really know how to dance it."

The girl laughed, and someone said it wasn't rock 'n' roll at all. Carlo slipped another record out of its envelope and put it on instead. Some more people started to dance.

"This is more like it," said Giordani, coming up to me.

"It takes time," said Carlo, winking at him.

A girl from my class named Gabriella came over. Her red hair fell over her shoulders and around her small, white,

[16]

freckled face. Everyone was staring at her because of the way her tight dress set off her slender figure.

"Hi, Enrica," she said, and launched into school gossip. She said that Signora Aiuti, mother of the teacher of the same name, had discovered a boy and girl kissing each other in the lavatories and made a big fuss over it.

"The little fools!" she exclaimed. "Why couldn't they do it outside? Everybody knows about it now, and they're being called the 'lavoratory lovers.' That Elisa's the homeliest creature. . . . I can't imagine what he sees in her."

Carlo put his arm around her waist, and they began to dance, very close. I emptied my glass and went over to the window. Outside it was still raining. The fast-falling drops glistened in the light of the swinging street lamp, and shadowy passers-by scurried along under their open umbrellas. Occasionally a car's headlights focused upon them before it glided on, splattering water behind it. In a house across the way some children were chasing each other around a brightly lighted room and a woman stood over a stove, intent upon her cooking.

"Want to dance?"

Carlo slid his arm around my waist and pulled me to him. He danced very slowly, without paying attention to the rhythm of the music; he was slightly overheated and rubbed his body against mine, with his eyes half-shut. We danced through two or three records in this close embrace, until someone suddenly turned off the light. A girl shrieked, and some people burst out laughing. Carlo pressed me to him more tightly than before and started to breathe heavily into my ear. Even through my wool dress I could feel the pressure of his body. At this point everyone danced in silence. Nothing could be heard but the scraping of shoes on the floor and the boys' heavy breathing.

"Now we're with it," said Giordani out of the darkness.

"I'll say we are," said Carlo with a low laugh, brushing his lips against mine.

"The house is ours," Giordani went on, "since my family's away. We must make the most of it."

Nobody seemed to be listening. Someone called out for wine and Giordani put on the light and went to get it. A girl followed him and came back a few minutes later alone, her cheeks blazing and her blouse in disarray.

"I found some brandy," she shouted, exhibiting the bottle. One of the boys snatched it from her and the others crowded around him, passing it from hand to hand. They drank right out of the bottle, burst into laughter for no good reason and slapped one another on the back.

"You can't have that," protested Giordani, but the bottle was half empty.

"What do you care?"

"My father will kill me if it's missing. He'd hidden it in his bedroom."

"That's a lie," said the girl, suddenly facing up to him. "It was in the kitchen."

"You're the one that's lying. You know perfectly well that when we fell onto the bed we found it under the pillow."

Everybody laughed. In the confusion the girl managed to get back the bottle, and Giordani grumblingly let her keep it. Carlo left me to go dance with Gabriella, rubbing up against her in exactly the same way he had against me. She put her cheek on his shoulder and he buried his face in her hair and whispered something into her ear.

I asked Giordani for the telephone and he went with me into the hall.

"Do you want the directory?" he asked.

"No."

He couldn't seem to make up his mind to go away. Hesitantly he put his hands on my hips and tried to pull me toward him.

[18]

"Let me alone!" I shouted.

He took his hands away and walked off, with his shoulders hunched over. I dialed the number and waited.

"Is that you, Cesare?"

"Yes. What's the matter?" It was he, but his voice sounded funny. "What is it?" he went on, making an effort to seem agreeable.

"I want to see you."

"I can't. Not today or tomorrow. I've got too much to do. You know it's very close to my exam. I'll call you as soon as I can."

"All right," I said, putting down the receiver.

As I thought about the sound of his voice I realized what was funny about it. He was in bed with a woman. He answered in exactly the same way when he was making love to me. But his fiancée, Nini, wasn't the kind to let him touch her before they were married. Who could it be?

It was all too easy for me to imagine the room which I knew so well. Most likely Cesare had just fallen asleep. And she was lying with her legs against his, asleep, or perhaps, like me, staring up at the ceiling. After he had put down the receiver he had looked at her to see whether she knew who had called. Then he had brushed his lips against her shoulder and shot a glance at the clock. He had decided it was time to go back to studying. Perhaps he had gone to make a cup of coffee. And his father had been sitting there in the kitchen, reading the newspaper, as agreeable as ever and indifferent to everything going on around him.

"What are you up to, Enrica?"

Carlo was there before I could notice. He grabbed my shoulders, wheeled me around and kissed me. He had narrow lips and there was an odor of Pernod upon them.

"Want to come with me?"

I followed him into the dark living room, where the dancing had stopped and people were petting in the corners. The

only light was that of the street lamp, which came diagonally through the windowpanes and created a feeble glow in
the vicinity of the window. The phonograph had been turned
down low. I caught a glimpse of Gabriella's hair against the
sweater of a bulky boy lying on the couch. She had pushed
off her shoes and was laughing hysterically.

"What's *her* trouble?"

"Too much to drink."

By this time Carlo had stopped dancing. He was pushing
me up against the wall as if he wanted to crush me, and kissing my ears and hair. Then he drew abruptly away.

"I'm fed up with it in here. Let's go out. Do you want to
come?"

"Go see if it's still raining."

He went over to the window and threw it open. I followed
him and stuck out my head. The rain seemed to have
stopped, but there was an agreeable wet smell. We picked
our coats out of the pile on a bed and left the house without
even saying good-bye. It was chilly outside and the damp air
stuck to us like wet gauze.

"I know a place where we can find some peace and quiet,"
said Carlo.

"Where's that?"

"Just keep going and you'll see."

My shoes were soaked with water, but I didn't feel cold.
At the street corner we were struck by a blast of wind. The
wet macadam reflected the passing cars and the shop windows. We walked side by side for what seemed a long time.
Cars sped by, with their tires sloshing through the water.
Carlo was staring straight ahead, with his hands in his coat
pockets and a gloomily intent air. I had a hard time keeping
in step. Every now and then he forged ahead and I had to
run to overtake him. My feet hurt and I was perspiring.

"Where are we going?"

"Never mind. I know."

[20]

He looked at me vacantly and quickened his pace. We went by a newsstand, with garishly colored magazines on display and I slowed down in order to look at them. But Carlo plowed straight on.

"Here we are," he said at last.

I looked around. We were on an unpaved street, riddled with holes. On one side there were the skeletons of two buildings under construction. Behind a fence there was a garden, heavily planted with greenery and flowers and drenched with rain.

"Now what?"

"Just follow me."

He looked around, then slipped a rail out of the fence and bent down to pass through.

"Isn't there anyone there?"

"No. This garden is going to be torn up to make way for the houses. But there's a night watchman on guard. Don't make any noise."

I made my way through the fence after him. The mud caused me to slip, and I had to catch on to the rails. Carlo signaled to me to keep quiet and follow. The leaves of the bushes stuck to my face, and in my mouth there was a taste of mingled water and pollen. Carlo walked unhesitatingly ahead, without pausing to feel his way. Every now and then he looked around to see if I was there.

"Come on! Make it snappy!"

Through the underbrush alongside the wall of one of the new houses I saw a little shack, which might have been a storehouse for lumber. We crawled in and found ourselves in a space barely large enough to turn around in. A wet mat covered the floor. Carlo sat huddled up as if all his strength had gone from him. His hands were trembling, and he couldn't manage to light a cigarette.

"Probably it's damp," I told him.

He shook his head and continued to throw away one

match after another until finally the cigarette was lit. He blew a mouthful of smoke into my face.

Now that the strenuous effort of the walk was over I felt cold and somehow disappointed. I had no urge to be any closer to Carlo but simply looked out through the open door into the garden. Water was trickling down the loose-jointed boarded walls of the shack. I pulled my coat tightly around me, but even so I felt soaking wet. Carlo threw away his half-smoked cigarette and started to massage my feet.

"Are you cold? Are you cold?" he repeated.

"No," I said, and I meant it. From my feet and legs I could feel the warmth rising. Suddenly he was on top of me and groping between his coat and mine.

"What a lot of clothes!" he said angrily, and then burst out laughing. He tugged so hard that one of my buttons flew off.

We made love in a hurry, impeded by our coats and the rest of our clothing. At the end Carlo slid down beside me with a sigh of satisfaction. He lit a cigarette and we took turns smoking it. The dampness was beginning to penetrate our clothes.

"Shall we go?"

"Yes."

As we crawled out of the low doorway we got our knees covered with mud. Carlo pulled me to him and gave me a kiss. We could hear only the crackling of the leaves under our feet and the horns of some distant cars. Carlo put his arm around my shoulders.

"What time is it?" I asked.

"Half-past eight."

"It's late. My mother's going to kick."

"Let her kick then."

Carlo walked toward the place where we had come in, and I followed. He took the rail out of the fence and put it back when we were out on the street. We stopped under a street lamp to examine our clothes.

"My God, what a mess!" Carlo grumbled. I looked at the caked mud on his back and his soaked shoes.

"You look like a wildcat with your wet hair all mussed," he observed.

"I don't know what *you* look like, but it's something very funny."

We exchanged a quick embrace and then ran to catch a tram which was just coming around the corner. The tram was full of tired, hungry office workers on their way home to dinner. I tied my scarf around my head in order to hide my disorderly mop of hair.

"Where do you live?" Carlo asked.

"Via Moroni."

"I'll see you home."

3

When I came into the house my father hid the bird cage on which he was working under the tablecloth. He spent all his time making bird cages. Each one took months to finish, and he was always cutting his hands on the wire. But the cages came out very well, equipped with everything they needed and a few extras besides. Only they didn't provide us with a living. That came mostly from my mother's work at the post office, because father's insurance company job was irregular and poorly paid.

"It's only me," I said.

At once his face relaxed. He uncovered the cage and held it up between two fingers.

"Do you like it?" he asked.

He had never made a cage quite so complicated. Around the central portion there were four towers, topped by cupolas, and on the cupolas tiny flags were flying.

"It's a beauty," I said, and he turned it around before my gaze.

"Do you really think so?" he asked, looking contentedly into my eyes. Then his face darkened. "I'm not so pleased, really," he said, laying it on the table. "It isn't strong enough, and the paint is one I've never used before; I'm sure it will crack. I simply must find another brand. But tell me, how do

[24]

you like the towers? Do you know how I happened to think of them? When I was looking at a picture of a Byzantine church in a book belonging to your mother, one of the books she had when she meant to be a school teacher. I want to show it to you."

He started to go get the book, but stopped in the middle of the room to listen to a noise coming from the stairs.

"There she is, right now," he said.

He hid the cage and went to fetch a sheaf of insurance papers.

"Will you help me fill out these blanks?" he asked.

"I have to cook supper," I replied.

"All right, all right." He let out a deep sigh and bent his head over the mass of numbers on the pages before him.

My mother noticed immediately that I was splattered with mud and asked me why. She was more nervous than usual and repeatedly fingered her hair. She opened her wet umbrella and set it in the hall. As she went into her room to take off her clothes and shoes she was still asking where I had been and what I had been doing.

"Cesare's no gentleman," she said, "or else he wouldn't have let you get soaked on the way home."

"I wasn't with Cesare. I went dancing in the house of a boy called Giordani."

"I don't believe it," she shouted as she stretched herself out on the bed. "My God, I'm tired!" Her voice was strained and strident. "That Cesare wants to get his hands on you, I wager. The rat! But I hope you haven't forgotten my advice. If he gets you in trouble I'll raise the roof. I'll go straight to that father of his—what's his name?—and force him to get the boy to marry you."

Her voice had gone flat, as if she were trying to convince herself rather than me of the truth of what she was saying. She yawned several times and closed her eyes. At least that is what I imagined, because I did not hear her stir.

I went into my own room and tried hard to scrape off the mud with a clothes brush. But it was still wet and clung to the wool. I hung up my coat in the closet and looked into the mirror at my red face and wild hair. As I rubbed my head with a towel I realized that I had the odor of Carlo upon me and I decided to take a bath.

I wanted to call Cesare, so I went to see if my mother was really sleeping. She was breathing heavily through her open mouth, so I closed the door. My father seemed to be absorbed by his figures, although probably he was dreaming of a new sort of bird cage, so I closed the kitchen door as well. Then I picked up the telephone and dialed Cesare's number.

There was no answer, and I imagined the house as dark and empty, with the usual smoky, moldy smell. Cesare's bed was always unmade, with a deep dent in the middle left by his body and, beside it, another shallower imprint left by a girl and a few wiry hairs. Cesare almost never opened a window; even in the daytime he preferred to study by the light of a lamp. He sat at his desk in his dressing gown, with his legs spread out and his big blond head bent over his books. The desk was in front of the wardrobe, and a mirror hung on one of its open doors. Sometimes Cesare stared at himself indefinitely with vacant, expressionless eyes. Every now and then, his father came in, when he knew that Cesare was alone, to make sure that he was studying; then, with a satisfied smile he went away, closing the door behind him.

Occasionally Cesare stared, instead, at the photographs of Holland, as intently as if he had never seen them before. He examined every detail and then decided to change their positions, hanging the one on top lower down and vice versa. In front of him, on his desk, there was a glass full of sharp-pointed pencils and two or three half-empty packs of cigarettes. At one side there was a bookcase where books were piled up in disorder. On the top shelf there were various geegaws: a tiny wooden seal, which might have been Dutch, a rag doll with a calendar hanging around its neck, a cowbell and a photograph of himself as a baby, lying stark naked on a couch.

With my ear glued to the receiver I listened to the distant ring, which seemed to come straight out of the tense contraction of the pit of my stomach and to travel over the wires all the way to Cesare's empty house. Still there was no answer. I hung up and returned to the kitchen. My father had gone back to his bird cage, but when he saw me he started.

"Oh, it's you, is it?"

I rolled up my sleeves and took a head of lettuce over to the sink to wash it. The water from the tap was icy cold and half paralyzed my fingers. From the floor above came the sound of chairs scraping the floor and a baby's desperate cry. My mother staggered, yawning, into the kitchen. Her face was pale and swollen and there were red circles around her eyes.

"I'm too tired," she said. "You'll have to fix your father's supper. I'll have a bowl of hot milk and go to bed."

"Very good."

My father, with his head inside the cage and a piece of wire between his teeth, looked up, without moving, as if in the expectation of some embittered remark. But my mother barely shot a glance in his direction, as if she were totally unconcerned with either his bird cages or his insurance papers. She poured some milk into a pan and put it on the gas. Her hands were trembling.

"Do you feel sick?" I asked her.

"No."

She stuck a finger into the milk and tested it. Then she wrinkled up her nose in disgust, peered into the coffee pot and poured its contents into the milk, adding a couple of spoonfuls of sugar.

"Can I bring it to you in bed?" I asked her.

[27]

"No; I'll do it myself."

I looked at her flabby profile, the caked mascara on her eyelids, her flat nose, pallid lips and the splotches of powder on her double chin. Her eyes were closed with fatigue, and the milk boiled up over the edge of the pan without her even noticing. She muttered a curse, turned off the gas and poured what was left of the milk into an earthenware bowl. Then, holding the steaming bowl in both hands, she started toward the bedroom.

"Good night," she said, without turning around.

My father raised his head, without speaking.

"When you come to bed, don't make any noise," she said, opening the door and shutting it, with a dull thud, behind her.

"Good night," I shouted.

Then I put the soup on the gas to heat it and went on washing the lettuce. With bright eyes and steady hands my father worked on his bird cage. He drilled holes in the wood, painstakingly blew away the dust and slipped in the wire. If the point was too big he took a file and, holding it between two fingers, filed first one side and then the other, blowing the filings away with his half-closed lips.

"If we had another bed, or even a couch, I'd sleep in here," he murmured all of a sudden. "That way I wouldn't disturb Teresa."

He was talking to himself rather than to me. If I had answered he would only have been annoyed and motioned to me to be silent. He didn't want his work interrupted.

"I'd be nearer my work, too," he went on, "nearer to this cage, I mean. If during the night I had some bright idea . . ." He raised his head and looked at me with a perplexed expression.

I began to set the table, right beside his tools, and he looked at my hands suspiciously, as if he imagined that I was trying to chase him away.

[28]

"Half the table is quite enough for the two of us," I said reassuringly.

"Of course," he said, laughing to himself. "There's plenty of room." And he looked down at the length of the table.

I fried two eggs and mixed the salad in a deep bowl. Then I put everything on the table, while my father went to wash his hands. He ate in silence, to the sound of the rain beating against the windows. Then the neighbors turned on their television and the confused sounds of "Double or Nothing" came through the walls. My father seemed not to hear. I lazily imagined the setup of the program and the conventional phrases with which it was unfailingly conducted.

"By the way, I was going to show you a book," said my father, and he went out into the hall, where our only bookcase was standing. In it were all the notebooks that my mother had kept during the two years she went to the university with the idea of becoming a teacher, four or five novels by foreign writers, a *Divine Comedy* bound in red leather and some outdated railway timetables. My father came back with the book in his hands. Slowly he leafed through it until he came to the photograph of a small redbrick Byzantine church with its cupolas, large and small. On the next page there was a picture of the inside, of white walls with traces of frescoes, of stars the size of gardenias and an enlarged, irregular sun.

"Just look how those cylindrical shapes fit one into the other. Look at those windows. They're placed in such a way as to create a rhythm. Not all of them are real windows, and that's why there's not more light inside. I went to Greece once upon a time, when my father was a young man and had business abroad. We traveled on donkeys, I remember, and I was scared. I must have been about nine years old; it was early in the century. I even remember a church—perhaps several churches—with that many cupolas. If only I could

[29]

reconstruct that shape for my bird cages . . . It's all a matter of the proportions."

His voice weakened and then died away as he lost himself in his memories. He nodded his head and looked down at his hands, which were roughened by the tools. I was sleepy and realized that it was too late for a bath. I heated some water in which to wash the dishes and put them in, together with a handful of soap powder.

"Good night, Father," I said when I had finished.

He did not even look up. I went away, leaving him with his memories, beside the big Byzantine bird cage.

4

Monday, and it was still raining. In the courtyard a woman was talking about the Flood. I got out of bed shivering and didn't stop to wash until I was fully dressed, when I held first one cheek and then the other under the cold water.

The bathroom windowpanes were clouded. With my finger I traced "Cesare," and then traced it again, upside down. In the beginning I hadn't liked the name; I thought it was pompous. Then, by degrees, I got used to it. Now I realized, all of a sudden, that it had acquired special connotations. When I saw it I thought of his slightly melancholy blond head. Cesare hardly ever smiled. He did so reluctantly and with a suddenly childish expression. His eyes, nose and forehead all smiled, but a second later his face darkened, as if he were ashamed of having let himself go.

"It's the Flood, I tell you!" repeated the voice in the courtyard. Then a radio on the floor above burst into noisy music.

When I came into the kitchen I saw that my mother had already had breakfast and was about to leave. She had jammed her old wine-red cloche over her eyes and, holding her gloves under her left arm, was sewing up a tear in her raincoat.

"Good morning," I said.

She raised her eyes and gave a faint smile.

[31]

"What a day!" she muttered. Then she bit off the thread and stuck the needle into the front of her dress. "There! That's done! I've got to hurry. Don't be late for school. I'll see you at two o'clock." She slipped on the raincoat and went out, slamming the door.

I heated up some coffee and dipped a slice of dry bread into it. Rain was streaming down the windowpanes, and outside it was as dark as night. The barracks building across the way had changed color; its usual pink surface was marred by violet splotches. I could see the rectangular courtyard in the middle; a soldier was running across it with a newspaper protecting his head. One of the windows blew open, and I heard a bugle playing a subdued marching air. I walked away from the window and looked idly at my mother's book, which had been left on the table the night before. Churches, frescoes, oil paintings. . . . My eyes fell on the Saint Jerome of Antonello da Messina.

"What are you looking at?" said my father's voice from behind, causing me to start. He ran his hand over the color illustration.

"Very beautiful," he said.

"It's Saint Jerome."

"Notice the light in the room, and the calm of the atmosphere. . . ."

He ran his fingers over the page as if they could feel the colors. His fingernails were black and broken, and his skin impregnated with dust.

"Here's a color that can't be the same in the original," he remarked, touching the saint's red cloak. "In the painting it must be livelier and less artificial, perhaps with an orange tinge."

"Shall I fix you a cup of coffee?" I asked him.

But he continued to stare at the book and made no reply. I poured the coffee, but he seemed not to notice that it was there. I slipped my two books and my notebooks under my coat and went out, closing the door noiselessly behind me.

The course in bookkeeping was given in a basement room. Because I was late I dashed at top speed down the cold, dark stairs, with my umbrella dripping on my legs. In the hall electric light bulbs were burning. From some of the rooms came a hum of typewriters, like that of a rushing mountain stream. I stopped in front of the door to catch my breath and then went in.

Signorina Aiuti shot me a bored glance and said nothing. I slipped silently into my seat. Gabriella gave me a sign of recognition. Carlo was sitting two rows ahead and continually turning around. His face was pale, and his dark hair fell over his forehead. Everywhere there was a smell of wet shoe leather. The blackboard was covered with numbers. The six lights were all on, but they looked like half blown-up balloons and provided little illumination. Dampness was practically dripping from the walls.

I pulled one of my notebooks, which was warm from contact with my skin, out from under my coat and started to write in it, according to Signorina Aiuti's instructions. Rumor had it that Signorina Aiuti had married an ex-prize fighter and that after a few months he had run away with her sister. After two years the fugitive couple had returned, and now the three of them lived in harmony together. Her face was yellow with powder; she had fine but inexpressive eyes, a wrinkle running across her forehead and a well-shaped mouth, with smooth, rounded lips. She called out the numbers in a sharp, almost harsh voice, making all sorts of faces in order to conceal her yawns. Carlo turned around and stared at me as if he had something to say. Gabriella was scribbling distractedly, pausing every now and then to examine her legs. Her red hair shone in the artificial light. When Signorina Aiuti had finished dictating Gabriella laid

[33]

down her pen and rolled her sleeves up over her freckled white arms.

"Take another sheet of paper. Can't you see that with that giant handwriting of yours one sheet isn't enough?"

Signorina Aiuti paced up and down among the benches, pausing to look over our shoulders. She wore her black hair knotted at the back of her head and held up with gilt hairpins. She continued to dictate problems, standing critically behind us until we had solved them and examining her lacquered nails. From the last row a girl asked her a question. She answered vaguely and went back to examining her nails, as if she were totally indifferent to us and to the course she was supposed to be giving. Actually it seemed as if her only ambition were to sleep. Gradually a protest arose from the back rows and the sound of it filled the entire room. Signorina Aiuti pretended not to hear. She went over to the window, leaned her forehead against the glass and stayed there, with her back turned to the class and her hands crossed behind her back. One of us dropped a notebook on the floor and she turned brusquely around. She paced up and down among the rows of benches and then went back to the platform, crossed her legs and lit a cigarette.

At ten o'clock I went up to the department of typing and stenography on the ground floor. Carlo and Gabriella were in the same class. We sat down in front of the typewriters, which were high, black, old-fashioned models, like locomotives. We were supposed to learn how to use all our fingers. To this end we wrote the same words over and over, words with two fingers, then with three, finally with all ten. The words were pronounced by a loudspeaker. The record contained not only words but also selected passages. We knew them by heart and nobody bothered to listen. All the typewriters started off together, with a great noise. Two teachers ran from one room to another, untangling typewriter ribbons and setting the students' hands in their correct place on the keyboard.

> *Benelli and Company, April 8, 1960. Benelli and Company, April 8, 1960, Milan.*

The loudspeaker repeated the phrase, adding something new.

I filled half a dozen pages with business letters. Then I let the teacher, who smelled of geranium soap, set my hands properly on the keyboard. I put the carbon paper in the wrong way around, so that my sheet came out typed on both sides. Gabriella laughed when she saw me throw it away and then wipe my ink-stained fingers on my skirt.

An hour later we went to still another room for our shorthand lesson. All during the period we scribbled on our long red-lined notebook pages. The shorthand teacher's name was Aiuti too; she was the mother of the one on the floor below, although they did not look at all alike except for the way they fixed their hair. Her narrow forehead and sharp nose gave her a birdlike appearance, but her small, far-away eyes were alert and gleaming. Her smiling mouth revealed two black holes between her teeth. Unlike her daughter, she was quite talkative and frequently sat down beside her pupils, patting their heads or arms.

"Your shoes are all wet and muddy," she said to me with a conciliatory smile. She was bored with teaching and would rather have listened to our life stories.

"What does your father do?" she asked Gabriella.

Gabriella looked at her with blank, astonished eyes and began to suck her pen.

"Is he well-off?" asked Signora Aiuti, leaning over until her lips brushed against Gabriella's hair.

Gabriella shook her head. Signora Aiuti made a face which seemed to indicate that it was too bad for Gabriella to be poor when she had such superb red hair. Then she walked away, rubbing her hands together on account of the cold.

At one o'clock the lights went out, and we all made a bee-line for our coats in the hall. Signora Aiuti was grumbling about the sudden darkness. "I can't see far enough to put one foot down in front of the other," she mumbled, catching on to the flying tails of a boy's coat. He tried to get away, but she held fast and they went down the stairs together. He was embarrassed and impatient, but her hand gripped him like a hook. At the bottom of the stairs the hall was crowded with people who thought that any minute it might start to rain.

"Three days it's rained already! There's no reason to think it'll stop now," said someone just behind me, giving a push to two girls who were shouting in loud voices as they made their way to the street.

Carlo came up. He had no raincoat and was carrying his books under one arm in such a way that they were visible under his jacket. An umbrella with a bamboo handle was hanging over one arm.

"Hi there, Enrica."

He stood on first one foot and then the other and didn't seem to know what to say. "Some weather!" he mumbled.

"Some weather, yes."

"Are you busy this afternoon?"

"Yes, I am."

"What about tomorrow?"

"I might be free."

"Shall I come by for you?"

"No. Give me a ring."

I opened up my umbrella and went out on the street. Water was splashing everywhere and my legs were soon soaking wet.

"I'm coming with you," said Carlo, starting to walk at my side.

5

My father, my mother and I sat down at the table. Outside it was still raining. My mother sucked up her spaghetti, spraying sauce on the tablecloth. My father was annoyed, but instead of making a remark he gave her an object lesson, patiently turning his fork until all the spaghetti was wound around it and then deftly conveying it to his mouth. But my mother paid no attention. She kept her eyes on the plate and went on chewing. After she had come home from work and put on her housedress, my mother's body collapsed. Losing all its shape and consistency, it draped itself over the chair like an empty sack.

When we had finished the spaghetti I brought on the meat. My throat was raw and burning. My father watched my mother apprehensively to see if she was taking the biggest piece of pork. I held out the platter, and he quickly transferred a slice to his plate and poured all the remaining sauce over it. Then, because he became aware that I was scrutinizing him, he paused, holding his knife and fork in midair, with a perplexed expression.

"Help yourself," he said, with a motion of his head. "I don't really care so much about the sauce."

My mother finished her portion and began poking at her teeth with a toothpick.

"I really ought to go to the dentist," she said, as she struck a sensitive spot.

We peeled our pears, each one of us concentrating upon the task, without raising our eyes from our plates.

"Turn on the radio, will you?" said my mother, pushing her chair back from the table.

My father shuddered. The radio jarred his nerves, but this was something my mother never seemed to remember. The telephone rang and I ran to answer.

"If that's Cesare, tell him that you have to study," my mother shouted after me. "Play hard to get."

I shut the kitchen door before taking the telephone off the hook.

"Enrica?"

"Yes. Who's this?"

"Carlo."

Silence.

"What's the matter? Am I disturbing you?"

"No. It's just that I was expecting someone else to call."

"Who's that?"

"Nobody you know."

"How about getting together this afternoon?"

"Nothing doing."

Silence. He breathed heavily into the telephone, as if he were expecting me to change my mind.

"So long," I said.

"So long, Enrica."

I went back to the kitchen, where my mother was clearing the table. To my surprise she was singing. She had a sweet, low-pitched voice, which I remembered from the time when I was a child and she used to sing me to sleep with old country songs.

"Oh God, what a backache!" she groaned. "Who was it?"

"Carlo. A boy from school."

"What's his father do? Has he got money?"

"I doubt it."

"None of your friends amounts to a hill of beans," she said bitterly. "A girl like you ought to be thinking about getting married. She should make herself hard to get, and be choosy about her friends. It's no use going around with people who serve no practical purpose. What's up with Cesare? Why doesn't he call?"

"Don't ask me."

My father was still mopping up the gravy from his plate. My mother snatched it away, but he said nothing. She put a cup and spoon in front of him and began filling the coffee pot with coffee. As she turned on the gas she clenched her dry lips, and I fancied I was looking at my own gestures when I should be her age, with my husband sitting in my father's chair in the same sort of smelly kitchen. A feeling of panic came over me. I stared at the window, where the rain-drops were shattered before they trickled down the panes. The telephone rang again and my mother started to go answer it, but I got there first.

This time it was Cesare. I saw a projection of his bored face on the wall. His voice was imperative at the other end of the wire.

"I'm coming to get you in the car," he said. "I feel like a drive. What do you say?"

"It's all right with me."

"I'll be there at four o'clock."

"So long."

My mother stared at me while I drank my coffee. She was breathing with difficulty, as if there were something stuck in her throat. For some time now she had been suffering from asthma. Whenever she was tired she became short of breath and red splotches appeared on her face.

"Who was that?" she asked.

"Cesare."

"It was about time! Is he coming to get you?"

[39]

"Yes."

"In his father's car?"

"Yes."

"Good," she said, approvingly. "But remember what I told you." She smiled unconvincingly, with a melancholy expression in her dark eyes.

My father had gone to sleep, with his head on his chest and his hands at his sides. Every now and then he moved one arm as if he were trying to find a more comfortable position.

"I'm going to lie down," said my mother, leaving the room and closing the door behind her.

I wasn't the least bit inclined to take an afternoon nap. The prospect of seeing Cesare had caused waves of heat to radiate through my body. I took out my notebooks and wrote in shorthand the first things that came into my mind. *"This is a wonderful day. I love you. I love you. I love you. Tomorrow's Thursday. It's raining. Your legs are covered with blond hairs. I'm sleepy. I'm not sleepy. I love you. . . ."* I filled two or three pages and then I began to feel cold. I pulled up the neck of my sweater and stuck my nose inside. It occurred to me that before going out with Cesare I ought to take a bath. I put down my notebook and went to turn on the hot water; then I shut the bathroom door and began to get undressed. Soon the air was filled with steam. As I took off my sweater I remembered what Cesare had said about it. It was old and faded, and when I held it up to the light I saw that in spots the wool was worn as thin as gauze. I threw it onto the floor and told myself I'd get a new one that very afternoon.

My mother insisted upon my wearing her discarded clothes, no matter how unbecoming. When she decided that one of her dresses was too small or too old she ripped out the seams and sewed them up again to fit me. Then she presented me with the dress as if it were brand-new. I hung it up in the closet with no intention of ever putting it on, and she never spoke of it again.

Now I eased myself into the hot water, with a feeling of calm and well-being. The bathroom was dense with steam and the heat penetrated my pores while the pungent smell of the soap stimulated my nostrils. Just then my mother came in to wash her hands.

"I'm going back to the office," she said, leaning over the tub and looking enviously at my soap-covered body.

"You'd better dress warmly," she said as she left.

I dried myself with the green-striped towel, redolent of perspiration, which had been hanging—God knows how long—for all of us to use, from a nail on the door. "This evening I'll wash it," I resolved as I sprayed myself with talcum powder. I got dressed in a hurry and went to my mother's room in search of some money. In one corner of a supposedly secret bureau drawer there were some three thousand liras. I took a thousand and locked the drawer. Then I went back to the living room.

"Father, have you got any money?"

He was asleep, and I had to shake him.

"What is it?" he asked, pulling himself together.

"Have you got any money? I want to buy a new sweater. The one I've been wearing is too far gone."

"What do you mean, money? I still owe the junk dealer two thousand liras for the material for the cage."

"Why don't you ever sell them, those cages of yours?"

"There don't seem to be any buyers. But if I could improve the system for opening them . . ."

Without waiting for him to finish I went to put on my coat and shoes. I couldn't bear the feel of my old sweater on my freshly washed and powdered skin. I went into the first shop I came to on the Piazza Bologna and asked to see all the sweaters they had in stock. Of course there was nothing for as little as a thousand liras. I told the shopkeeper how much money I had, and she looked at me suspiciously.

"There isn't anything at that price," she said, but after a

moment's reflection she told me to wait. She went into a back room and returned with a box under her arm.

"These are some sweaters I'm supposed to send back because they're imperfect. If one of them appeals to you . . ."

The sweaters were all black, with low necks.

"I wanted a bright color," I said.

"These don't show the dirt," she replied, persuading me to feel the wool with my fingers.

"All right," I said. "I'll take one. In fact I'd like to put it on right away." And I dodged behind a cabinet to make a quick change.

One of the sleeves was longer than the other and the size was definitely too large. But I had no choice. I rolled up the sleeves, put on my coat, slapped the money on the counter and left.

6

Cesare was waiting in front of the house, at the wheel of his father's Fiat 600.

"Next time you're late you won't find me," he said by way of greeting. Then he opened the door so that I could get in beside him and started the motor.

I looked at his profile, outlined against the window, at the small, sensual nostrils, the shiny cheeks covered with blond fuzz and the heavy, almost white eyebrows. He leaned over the steering wheel and drove on without speaking. I felt as if he were quite detached from me, like a part of the motor. When we were outside the city he started to relax. He turned once to look at me, but without saying a word. Then he took my hand and put it on his thigh. At a certain point he veered off onto a narrow road and slowed down the car. The road was not paved, and the wheels jolted from one hole into another, spraying mud. On one side there were bluish green fields with a few scattered olive trees, on the other a ditch, where a muddy stream made its way between clumps of grass and thorny bushes. Cesare brought the car to a halt in an open space, with the rear wheels on the grass.

"I don't want to get stuck in the mud," he explained, getting out and walking around the car in order to examine the wheels more closely. "The ground's fairly hard," he said. "It'll hold up."

Then he got back into the car, unbuttoned his coat and lit a cigarette. The rain began to come down harder than ever, bouncing like pebbles on the roof of the car.

"I like it when it's raining," I said.

"I don't."

He leaned over to kiss me. His lips were dry, and his mouth had a taste of hot coffee. I slipped off my coat, pulled the sweater more tightly across my breasts and rolled up the overly long sleeve. But Cesare didn't seem to notice that the sweater was new. He tried to push the seat back, but the spring was caught and wouldn't move. He turned toward me and took my head in his hands. I felt the warmth of his fingers on my cheeks and a creeping desire for his body. I told him so, and he smiled, raising my skirt and sliding over on top of me with his legs curled up under the steering wheel and his head against my shoulder. I let him push me backward, although the handle of the door was sticking into my side. His hands groped impatiently under my skirt. Finally he penetrated me, while his teeth sank into my neck. When we drew apart my temples were still pulsing. It was dark outside. Every now and then a car went by, with its headlights falling momentarily upon us before it disappeared around the curve. Cesare got out and came back, soaking wet, a minute later.

"It's still raining," he said.

He switched on the roof light and looked at himself in the mirror. His hair was in disorder and his shirt rumpled and stained with perspiration. As I tried to arrange my own clothes I had a burning sensation in my cheeks, and a pain in my neck.

"What a messy business in the car! I swear I'll never do it again."

"Why didn't we go to your house?"

"Do you really want to know? Because my father wanted

[44]

to be alone. He has his women, too. He threw me out, damn him!"

I leaned my head against his shoulder, and he silently lit a cigarette. What with the monotonous dripping of the rain and the warmth of his body, this time I was the one who nearly fell asleep.

"Let's go," he said brusquely, tossing the cigarette butt away. "I've got to study this afternoon and tonight too."

He gave me a last kiss on the cheek and started the motor. There was hardly any visibility. The light thrown by the headlights was swallowed up in the darkness, and the car moved through a curtain of water. Inside it was excessively warm; hot air from the motor surged up under our legs. Cesare drove very fast the whole way, amusing himself by passing all the more cautious drivers.

"Here you are," he said, drawing up in front of my house. "So long."

"Will you call me up?"

"These days I'm going to have to study. I don't know when we can get together."

"So long," I said, pausing to watch him splash around the corner and lose himself in the traffic.

The rain was pouring down my neck. At the foot of the stairs I paused, feeling slightly groggy because of the overpowering smell of fried fish. I sat down on one of the bottom steps and stared at the raindrops blowing against the streetlamp outside. The protective white glass plate was broken on one side, as jaggedly as if someone had bitten into it, and the bulb looked as if it might give out any minute.

Suddenly I saw my mother coming unsteadily toward me, clutching with both hands the purple umbrella she had carried for the last ten years. I looked at my watch. For her this was unusually early. She almost always did overtime and got home no sooner than eight-thirty. Now she looked in my direction but failed to see me. She shook the rain out of her umbrella and made up her mind to climb the stairs. Even when she walked past me she failed to notice that I was there.

"What are you doing here?" I said, causing her to start.

"I couldn't take it any longer. I had to ask for permission to come home."

Her face was drawn and the lipstick was caked on her wrinkled lips.

"Do you want to lean on me going up?"

"No, I'll make it."

I went ahead and lit the light in our front hall. My father must have gone to the insurance office. The bird cage stood under the kitchen table, covered with the torn sheet which we used to cover the ironing board. My mother threw herself on the bed, without having even enough energy to take off her clothes.

"Help me undo my brassière," she said after a few minutes. "It's so tight I can't breathe."

I helped her undress. I took off her dress and hung it in the closet, as I had seen her do so often. I pulled off her shoes and slip. Then I got her to sit on the edge of the bed while I slipped off her stockings. Her legs were swollen and covered with goose flesh because of the cold. She was breathing heavily, her breast rising and falling as if she could not get enough air.

"The brassière . . . Hurry!" she said.

I unfastened the hooks, one after the other, and her breasts, with the dark nipples, sagged onto her stomach. I couldn't seem to get the brassière completely loose. The elastic was frayed and lumpy, and her flesh bulged out on either side.

"Hurry," she gasped, and as she spoke she slipped out of my arms and, before I could catch her, she had fallen to the floor, with her head swinging against my legs. I tried to lift her up, but without success; she was too heavy. Finally I threw a blanket over her and went to call the woman who lived on the floor above us.

She clattered down the stairs in her slippers, bombarding me with questions. Once we were inside she helped me to take off the brassière and raise my mother onto the bed. Then she knelt down and began to sob under her breath. For a second I thought that my mother must be dead; then I saw that she was breathing, and I went into the kitchen to prepare supper. Soon after this my father arrived on the scene. He had a bag of peanuts in one hand and was munching some as he came through the door.

"Mother's in a bad way," I told him.

He paid no attention but picked up his cage and turned it deliberately around in his hands. He went into the bedroom to take off his coat and returned with a panicked expression.

"What's the matter?"

"I don't know. She fainted."

"We must call a doctor," he said.

"The office will send one."

"Oh, yes, of course."

He took his place at the table, sitting perfectly still and staring at the wall. I poured some soup into his bowl and cut him a couple of slices of bread. Then I sat down beside him.

"You forgot the wine," he said.

There was a small amount left at the bottom of the bottle, and he added it to his soup.

"It's cold," he observed.

The silence that followed was oppressive, and I turned on the radio. My father signaled to me to turn it off, but I pretended not to notice, and he shrugged his shoulders in resignation. He lifted the soup spoon to his lips and sniffed the smell of mingled grease and wine.

"Mmmm!" he said. "That's good."

[47]

The woman from the floor above came back later to see how my mother was doing. She too said that a doctor should be sent by the office.

"I'll call up. Don't you worry," she said, giving me a compassionate look before she went back upstairs.

7

My mother stayed in bed for several days. The doctor said it was nothing serious, just a matter of being over-tired, and prescribed shots. She didn't seem to be convinced by his diagnosis, but neither did she contradict it. When I was out, the woman from the floor above came to keep her company. She lay there, on her back, absorbed in the difficulty of breathing, and the visitor sat at the foot of the bed, knitting. My father didn't want to sleep in the same bed, so we borrowed a mattress from upstairs and he slept in the kitchen. Apparently this new arrangement pleased him.

Every morning they called up from my mother's office for the latest news, and one day they sent her flowers. I went to school as usual, and in the afternoon I was busy around the house. Once I went out to have a hot chocolate with Carlo. He was constantly calling me and asking me to go with him to the shack where we had gone before. I said I didn't want to, but he kept right on asking. Twice I called Cesare, but he wasn't home. His father's voice was hypocritically pleasant.

"Cesare's not here. Is that you, Enrica? I imagine he's gone to a friend's house to study. No, I haven't the slightest idea when he'll be back. I'll tell him that you called. Why haven't you been to see us?"

During her good moments my mother asked about Cesare. She wanted to put her finger on something definite.

"You ought to have a talk with that boy; I mean it. It's all wrong to drag out an engagement this way. If he doesn't mean to marry you, then he should give you your freedom. You're young and pretty, and you'll find somebody else."

Then she broke off and caught her breath.

"I don't know what there is in my throat. It feels all swollen."

She let her head fall back on the pillow and half closed her eyes. Without make-up her face actually looked younger. Gray hairs mingled with the black, and her head seemed smaller because it was sunk in the pillow.

"You bought a new sweater," she said one day as I sat at the foot of her bed, reading a picture magazine.

"I thought you'd fallen asleep."

"I can't seem to. . . . How much did it cost you?"

"A thousand liras."

"Did you take the money out of my drawer?"

"Yes, I did."

"With all the clothes you have in your closet, you have to go and get something new! And black, at your age! . . . It makes you look old."

"I didn't have any choice."

She shut her eyes again and turned her head to one side. I wondered if I could open the window but decided against it and went back to looking at my magazine, reading one sentence over and over without understanding. Finally sleep overpowered me. My head fell onto my chest, and I dreamed of my mother walking in the rain and clutching her purple umbrella as if it were a life jacket.

My father came into the room and asked me to fix dinner. He said he was hungry. I got up and started to leave the room. My mother muttered something, and I turned around. But I saw that her eyes were shut and her mouth open, so I went on into the kitchen. While I was putting the dinner together I listened to the television next door. A man was going on, insistently, about politics. Then he said that the three-day rain had caused floods at some place—I didn't catch the name. Such and such a member of the Cabinet had hurried to the scene. A road had given way, carrying two automobiles with it. Eight people were dead, and the Cabinet member had gone to condole with the families. These statements were underlined with appropriate music. Then he talked about soccer. He said that the international match was going well. The Italians were in the lead. I turned on the water in the sink full blast in order to cover the noise of the TV. My father signaled to me to turn the water off, and I did so just before bringing the food to the table. As soon as we had finished he picked up the cage and started to work on it, while I went to wash the dishes. After that I went to see if there was anything I could do for my mother. She was wide awake, with some pillows piled up under her back.

"Are you feeling better?"

"Yes, I am."

"Would you like something to read? A book or a paper?"

"No, thanks."

I left her and went to make a telephone call in the hall.

"Cesare?"

"Hello. How goes it?"

"What about doing something tomorrow?"

"I can't do it tomorrow. I'll call you next week."

"So long, then."

"So long."

I went to my room. It was cold. I looked out of the window and saw that it had stopped raining. There was a sliver of moon in the sky, as shiny as the blade of a knife. My bed had two broken springs and sagged on one side. I wondered if my father would be able to fix it. I sat down on the bedspread and looked through an old magazine. I felt very much awake and had an urge to go out. I went to see what my father was doing. As usual he was working on his cage. I told him that I was going out, but he made no reply. I looked into my mother's room and saw that she was sleeping quietly, with one hand on her chest.

Outside I was struck by a blast of cold air. I walked down the middle of the street, in order to avoid the raindrops which were still dripping from the trees. Quite involuntarily I walked in the direction of Cesare's house. A man went by, then fell back and followed me.

"Need money?" he asked, in a subdued, feminine voice.

I went on walking. He stopped for a moment, in perplexity, and then caught up with me again.

"So young!" he exclaimed. "Where are you going?"

I walked on without paying attention to what he was saying. He continued to follow me, but he was so remote from my thoughts that I didn't even notice when he went his own way. When I reached Cesare's house I came to a halt, feeling unsure of what I wanted to do. Slowly I walked around the corner and stopped in front of the flower vendor's stall to wait—what for, I didn't know. Very few people were out. In Cesare's house and the other houses near by the shutters were closed, and the general effect was one of emptiness. Cesare's apartment was on the top floor. The concierge must have just closed the outside door. On it there was a blue ribbon, to show that one of the tenants had given birth to a baby boy. I leaned up against the florist's stall. From between the boards came an odor of flowers.

A gang of noisy boys passed by, all of them talking at once and gesticulating. They took no notice of me at all. After them came an old woman, bent double under the weight of a shopping basket and mumbling indistinctly to herself. The street was a traffic artery, and cars buzzed rapidly by.

In the crack of the door of Cesare's house I saw a gleam of light. Three well dressed people—two men and a woman—

came out, and I thought I recognized Cesare among them. The men were wearing dark blue suits and the woman a bright green coat, as wide as a bedspread. In the doorway the two men started to talk between themselves, and the woman pirouetted before them. Then all of them burst into laughter. The man whom I had mistaken for Cesare took the woman by the arm and made as if to carry her away. The other man ran after and laughingly threw his arms around them. Then they all got into a streamlined white car which drove off and disappeared at the end of the street. I resigned myself to going away. I tied my scarf around my head, took a last look at the blue ribbon on the door and started back home.

8

A few days later my mother went back to her office. She said that she was well, but she seemed to be continually short of breath. After she had conveyed a forkful of spaghetti to her mouth, her eyes seemed to burst from their sockets and she rushed over to the window, threw it open and stuck her head out to gasp for air. My father protested that the room was too cold.

"Go get my overcoat," he grumbled.

My mother lingered at the window, as if to absorb as much air as she could. Then she came back to the table, buttoning her blouse up around her neck. My father snorted and signaled to me to go close the window. I closed it, but my mother was so taken up with her own thoughts that she didn't notice. When she had had her after-dinner coffee she returned to the window, opened it again and leaned out, resting her panting breast on the sill. My father warmed his hand on the coffee pot and shook his head disapprovingly.

At this point my mother no longer questioned me about Cesare. It was all she could do to go on living. When she came up the stairs she paused on every step and pressed her hand against her chest. She kept her mouth hanging open in order to breathe more freely. But she had no pain. The housekeeping fell upon my shoulders, and it left me very little time to myself. In the middle of the day, on the way back from school, I did the marketing; in the late afternoon I had to wash, iron and clean, and in the evening there was another meal to be prepared. Sometimes the woman on the floor above came down to help me. I left a pile of dirty clothes for her to do, and she made a quick job of them. Whenever I was able to persuade her to stay a little longer I got her to change my mother's sheets and mop the floor. Carlo called me up every day. And in the morning, when I started out for school, I often found him waiting at the downstairs door.

"What are you doing here?" I asked him.

"I wanted to see you, that's all."

"You knew you'd see me at school."

"Oh well, we go the same way, don't we?"

I admired his broad, serene forehead. His long, thin legs enabled him to take giant strides, and it was all I could do to keep up.

"Have you done your homework?" he asked.

"No, I haven't."

"Signorina Aiuti is in a bad mood. She enjoys handing out low marks."

"I thought she was bored with the whole thing."

"Perhaps it's a way of overcoming her boredom."

On the tram he brushed my breasts with his arm. If there was a crowd he shielded me with his body, leaning over to whisper something into my ear and giving me a kiss.

"No," I said decisively.

He scowled and looked away, with a gesture of annoyance. Then he looked at me again, waiting to see if I would change my mind. At school everybody said we were engaged. Gabriella knew better, but she said nothing. Sometimes I saw her go over to Carlo, with an indifferent expression, and bend down to ask him a question, with her flaming red hair falling around his face. Carlo pretended not to notice. Signorina

[55]

Aiuti paced up and down the room, looking vastly bored with the lot of us. Only occasionally did she sit down at the desk, and then she pulled a nail file out of her handbag and filed her nails. Sometimes we heard the footsteps of her mother on the floor above. On such occasions she raised her head, made a face and resumed her pacing. She made her explanations as short as possible and left us to grapple with the book.

"It's all there in the text," she said. "Read it for yourselves."

When she questioned us individually she did look at us, or rather she looked through us, with her eyes on something beyond the door. She nodded assent to our reply and then sent us back to our desks without any comment, so that we were never quite sure that she had been listening. Sometimes she leafed through a newspaper, looking up abruptly to ask:

"Well, why have you stopped? Go on."

"That's all I remember."

"Then go back to your seat. I've no time to waste."

Gabriella was dozing, with her chin cupped in her hand. Signorina Aiuti could not help noticing, but she made no remark. She stared down at her nails, with a bitter wrinkle around her lips. Two hours later her mother made a great fuss over us. There was nothing she wouldn't talk about, including her daughter, whom she accused of being eccentric.

"I have two daughters," she told us, "but I might just as well not have any. They never open their mouths. That poor husband! . . . He's like a puppy-dog between two statues. He makes me laugh. Poor fellow! He's overweight, and a very sick man. What can they see in him? I'm sure I don't know. They've been that way ever since they were little girls. Whatever one did the other copied; otherwise there was trouble. Mute and mulish, that's what they are. Two pieces of hard luck I didn't deserve. To my married daughter I'm always saying: 'You at least give me a grandchild!' But there's no chance of that. Among other things she's sterile. And her sister has never married. That's God's punishment for their hardheartedness. . . ."

She broke off, fearful of having said too much, and shook her head. But she couldn't be quiet for long. After a few minutes she raised her head and went on talking about the married daughter and her husband. Gabriella found it amusing to listen for a few minutes; then she began, absentmindedly, to scribble on the bench in front of her with her pen.

Carlo had changed seats. He was sitting directly behind me, and I thought I could feel his eyes on my neck. We went home together. To keep up with him I had to dogtrot, with my scarf around my face to keep my hair from blowing. We went by the big shoe shop, which was always crowded with customers, and the Olympia Bar, with its four doors open on the street and its windows piled high with cakes and stuffed animals. Sometimes we stopped to drink a hot chocolate. The mirror behind the bar sent back the reflection of his long, slender neck and my small, dark-skinned face. Carlo smiled at my reflection, and I hid my face behind my cup.

"I like being with you," he said.

We went away with a pleasantly warm feeling in our throats and ran for the bus.

My father complained that the house wasn't the way it used to be; his shirts weren't properly ironed, his shoes were left dirty and the spaghetti was undercooked.

"It seems as if we'd gone back to the time of the war," he said.

I shrugged my shoulders. There was always more than I had time to do about the house. Every day my mother lost ground. She forgot to put on her stockings or make up her face. As for her brassière, she had left that off ever since the day when she had fainted away. She went to the office bundled up in an old black dress, whose hemline hung low in the back, with her coat thrown over her shoulders and the usual felt cloche on her head.

"All day long I'll be making out bills," she said one morning, with a grimace of pain.

"Why don't you take a week off?" said the woman from the floor above, who was helping her down the stairs.

"They can't do without me. I've been there fifteen years."

"You poor thing!"

"I'll be entitled to my holidays in June, and then I can go somewhere in the mountains. But everything's so expensive."

Her voice was pitifully hoarse and unsteady.

"She's not well," I said to my father.

"The doctor says it's nothing serious," he retorted. "Only fatigue."

"He may be right," I said, without conviction.

"Something's wrong inside here," my mother said one day, touching her chest.

My father shot her a fearful glance and then went on with his lunch, dipping a piece of bread in the sauce.

"Is there any more spaghetti?" he asked me.

I gave him what was left.

"This evening you'd better give me some stewed prunes. I'm a bit clogged up."

"Yes, Father."

9

Thursday. When I came home I found that my mother had been taken to the hospital, and my father had gone with her. I followed as fast as I could, but the hospital was at the other end of the city and when I got there she was dead. Two Sisters were leaning over the bed where she was lying, and they offered me a chair. My father stood trembling in his overcoat in one corner, talking to himself.

"We must take her home," I heard him mutter.

White figures went to and fro, talking in loud voices.

"She had a good death," one of the Sisters whispered in my ear. "She received Extreme Unction. And she never complained."

The sun pouring in through the window lit up my mother's relaxed, putty-gray face. Her eyes were half-closed, but seemed to be looking out from under the lids. They had crossed her hands on her breast, but they were the hands of someone who had clung desperately to the sheets in the effort to draw breath. Beside the pillow there was an emerald-green oxygen mask with a silvery air capsule. And a smell of alcohol and ether hung over the bed.

A fly lit on my mother's forehead. I stared at her hands, waiting for them to make the gesture of brushing it away. On the floor above someone was screaming. The gray-tiled floor was flooded with sun. From the two rows of beds lined up on either side of the ward the other patients stared at us with frank curiosity. I don't remember how long we stayed there, looking at my mother. I hardly noticed when they carried her away and led my father and myself down the stairs and onto the street.

The next thing I knew I was at home, sitting in the same position as in the hospital, at the foot of the bed where my mother's dead body was lying. But the sun had set, and someone had lit the naked light which hung from the center of the ceiling. In front of me I saw a pair of shoulders shaken by sobs, which belonged to the woman who lived on the floor above. She had tied a kerchief around her head, just as when she did the cleaning. Under the knots I caught a glimpse of her handsome, muscular neck bent in prayer. My father had fallen asleep, with his chin on his chest. It occurred to me that I should have made him a cup of broth, but I didn't feel like taking the trouble. I gave in to my sleepiness, half enjoying the strange sensation afforded me by the presence of my mother's inanimate body. She didn't know that I was looking at her, I reflected; she'll never know. There is no relationship between us. I'm looking at her, and she doesn't know.

The sound of footsteps aroused me. Several neighbors had come in, and also a relative, a cousin of my mother whom we hardly knew. They kissed me on the forehead, and my cousin gingerly laid a bouquet of flowers at her feet. The woman from the floor above took a knife, cut the string around the flowers and scattered them over the body.

"Her office will pay the funeral expenses," said my cousin, not without a certain satisfaction. "I went there to see about it myself. When you're dealing with that kind of people you have to take a firm stand."

He raised his hand to his mouth and coughed, in the subdued manner that is appropriate in the presence of a dead body. He twirled his hat in his hands, not knowing where to put it down. Then he took off his gloves and stuffed them into his pockets. I caught a glimpse of the gold teeth that glimmered between his fleshy lips. After a short while the neighbors went away. The woman from the floor above embraced me and said that she would be back later.

My father was still sleeping, and my cousin asked me whether I thought we should wake him. I noticed that he had the same heavy, round head as my mother. His body, on the other hand, was thin. He was wearing a freshly starched white shirt and a black tie.

"I'll stay here and keep watch with you," he said.

I answered that that was not at all necessary. He patted my shoulder and insisted that he would stay all night. I didn't dare contradict him and went to get a chair. He turned off the light and sat in the darkness. It was black outside. The light from the streetlamp came through the window and fell upon the bed. The flowers seemed to spring out of the sheet and twine themselves around my mother's body. From them there came an almost disgustingly sharp, sweet smell, reminiscent of that which might have stemmed from the corpse. My cousin tried to distract me by talking about the land he owned near Frascati.

"There were a lot of grapes this year," he said, cocking his head and staring at me out of his beady, black eyes. "The only drawback was too much rain. The grapes are watery and there won't be enough alcohol or sugar in the wine. We'll have to mix it with some from the south."

All of a sudden my father got up and slipped into the kitchen. I realized that he must be hungry. After a few minutes I went to see if there was anything I could do. I found him kneeling on the floor and filing the door of his bird cage.

"Would you like some soup?" I asked. But he was holding some tiny nails between his teeth and did not reply.

When I went back in the other room I found my cousin praying over my mother's body. He did not turn around when I came in but finished his prayer and went back to where he had been sitting.

"Will you have something to eat?" I asked him.

"Not just now. Perhaps later on."

We sat in silence, with our eyes turned toward the bed. The woman from the floor above had spread out the bed cover under the body. It was a rectangle of richly embroidered satin which had belonged to her trousseau. There were clusters of fruit, in two colors, and white cherubim against a pale blue ground. The border had a design of golden sheaves of grain, and a long fringe fell to the floor. I found it hard to think of my mother in this new guise. Was I supposed to be waiting until her blood ran cold? Perhaps it was frozen and stagnant already. Her body seemed at times to be made of plaster, at others of papier-mâché. It must have been very light . . . or perhaps very heavy. It didn't make sense to think of her this way. I shut my eyes and thought of how she used to look when she went about the house, her face heavy with fatigue. Then I tried to imagine what she was like when she was young. But I couldn't. I asked my cousin to tell me something about the time when they were children together.

"Until we were eight years old we lived in the same house," he began. But that was all he had to say.

I tried to imagine her with a chubby child's body. Her hair must have been a rich golden brown; perhaps she wore a pigtail down her back and uncombed bangs low over her forehead. Then I saw her as a slender little thing in a shapeless dark blue smock, her legs splattered with mud, playing all alone with some pebbles. No, that was me. My mother must have been quite different. I couldn't really imagine her at all.

At a certain point I must have fallen asleep, because I dreamed I was inside my father's cage. It was wide and comfortable, but I was thirsty and couldn't find anything to drink. My father was looking at me from the outside, pleased with his architectural efforts. "What am I to do?" I pleaded. "You're perfectly well off exactly where you are," he answered, with tiny nails trickling out of his mouth. I sat down on the bottom of the cage and looked up at the ceiling. It was just like the cupola of a church. Then I discovered, with terror, that I wasn't in the cage, but in my mother's belly, which was as cold as a church and heavy with the smell of flowers.

I woke up and saw that, across from me, my cousin was sleeping. He sat quietly with his hands folded as if in prayer. I tiptoed out to the kitchen to make a cup of coffee. I drank it very hot and felt better. I went to my room to get my slippers. When I came back I found my cousin standing at the open window.

"It was stifling in here," he remarked.

"But now it's going to be cold. . . ."

He shrugged his shoulders and did not reply. Between his fingers he was holding a cigarette. He blew the smoke out the window and its cloud dissolved in the inky blackness of the night. There was no moon and only a few tiny stars were visible, like holes in a dark curtain.

"Will you give me one of your cigarettes?" I asked him.

"Of course . . . excuse me."

He held out the newly opened package, and a second later a lighted match.

"You're at school, I suppose," he said.

"Yes, I'm taking stenography and bookkeeping."

"When will you be through?"

"In two months."

"Then I suppose you'll look for a job."

"Yes."

"Unless you get married."

"Yes, unless I get married."

"Be sure to marry someone that can support you. When

two poor people join forces, it never works out. The lack of money ruins everything."

"Yes, I know."

"Have you someone in view?"

"No, I haven't."

"Too bad."

I noticed that he had the broad, gnarled hands of a peasant, but the head of a city dweller, with a smooth brow, drooping cheeks and a receding chin. He had very little hair, and what he had was painstakingly combed over around his shiny bald pate.

Once more I mentally pursued the image of my mother when she was young. She had spoken to me once about her family and how they had prospered on the land some time ago. They had been poor peasants at the start, until they made money out of trafficking of some kind or other during the first World War. Then they went back to being poor. Of the five brothers and sisters, three were dead. My mother had come to Rome on her own to study. Then she had got married and her ambitions came to nothing. Her only living brother had gone to America and no one knew what he was doing. The persevering cousins had stayed on the land and little by little recuperated their fortune. They were comfortably off and independent. She spoke of them with scorn. They had resented her ambitions, and she despised their attachment to the soil. Now that she was dead they had sent the youngest among them to keep watch over her body. The chances were that I would never see any of them in the future. Probably the flowers came from their garden. Or perhaps they had no garden, and the house was surrounded by vineyards and olive trees, or by fields of clover and alfalfa for the livestock, with parsley growing in flowerpots on top of the wall around the pigpen and chickens cackling in the barnyard.

I wished I knew where Cesare might be. He hadn't called

me for four days. The last time I had seen him was Sunday. We went to his house, but he sent me away in a hurry, as soon as we'd finished making love. His father had smiled at me as if to apologize for his son's thorny character, grasping my hands and holding them for a long time in his.

My cousin blew his nose. He smoked one cigarette after another, staring dreamily at my mother's body as if he did not really recognize it. He must have been hungry. It was almost morning. The barracks across the way had taken on a rosy hue and the cat had stopped meowing. I went to the kitchen and brought him back a cup of hot milk.

"Drink this," I said, "it will warm you up."

He thanked me and took the cup in both hands. He drank very slowly, with his nose and forehead practically in the saucer. When he had finished, he wiped his mouth with the back of his hand and gave the cup back to me.

"When Teresa was a little girl, she used to milk the cows. I used to peek through the wall of the barn, and in order to shock me she would take a cow's udder between her lips and let the milk pour down her throat. She was so rough that the cow mooed with pain. Strong as a man, she was! No one ever dreamed she'd go off to study in Rome."

He sighed, looked down at his dusty shoes and then hid them under the chair. He was faced with an hour's journey in the bus to get home, and the prospect of losing the crease in his black trousers. Now he adjusted his shiny black tie and opened his mouth in a yawn.

"I'd better be leaving," he said. "I'll be back for the funeral."

"I'm coming to the door," I said, and on the threshold I held out my hand.

"Good-bye."

"Good-bye, and thanks for keeping me company."

He went down the stairs two steps at a time. Then from

[65]

the landing he called up to me to make his farewells to my father.

"I will, don't worry."

"Good-bye, then."

And I never laid eyes on him again.

10

My father didn't want to be bothered with anything. Once his cage was finished he started on another, as big as a wardrobe, which occupied his entire attention. He had made a preliminary drawing, with all the measurements in their exact proportions, almost as if it were for a house.

Fortunately, the woman from the floor above came to my aid, for I hadn't the slightest idea what to do. She spoke with my mother's supervisor, ordered a coffin, with heavy gilt handles, and two flower pieces, one large and one small, and hired a hearse. She walked around our house as if it belonged to her. She wore a white kerchief around her head and her arms were bare, ready to clean up where necessary or to take over the telephone and call my mother's office or the undertaker. My father looked on her with suspicion, but he was grateful to her for letting him alone. She poked her nose everywhere except into his cage.

I had gone back to school and was spending as little time as possible at home. Present at the funeral were my father and I, the woman from the floor above, two women from the office, who had sent a green wreath ahead of them, and, at the last minute, Carlo. The hearse stood in front of the door. There were gilt angels on the corners of the chassis and the interior was lined with satin. Two men pushed the coffin inside, knocking its lid against the open door. The driver stood looking on, with his cap in his hand. There was a red mark, left by the cap, on his forehead.

After the two men had deftly and silently closed the door, the driver put his cap back on his head and took his place at the wheel. We walked behind the hearse, stamping our feet on the ground because they were cold. There was a biting wind which went right through our clothes. My father's face was blue and he kept blowing his nose.

"He'll get a chill," the woman from the floor above whispered into my ear. And she added a minute later: "Are you very sad? She was a wonderful woman, your mother. She thought of everything. Did you know that she had taken out a life insurance policy? That way there's something for you and your father to live on, not much, but it's better than nothing at all. Otherwise, with that good-for-nothing"—she nodded toward my father—"you'd be in a pretty mess."

At that very minute I noticed that she was wearing my mother's black coat. She followed the movement of my eyes and made an evasive gesture.

"Were you looking at the coat? I really should have said something about it before. I thought it was due me for all the work I've done in your house. You don't mind, do you?"

I shook my head. She smiled smugly and thrust her hands into the pockets. Probably she'd taken my mother's new kid gloves as well.

It was ten o'clock when we reached the cemetery. The wind was blowing harder than ever. The dried-up flowers on the graves were blown up into the air and fell apart, forming a cloud of dust. There were few people about, except for some women who seemed to be searching for something among the graves. The coffin was lowered into the ground, and we all made the sign of the cross. One of the undertaker's men threw away the cigarette butt which he had been smoking and began to toss shovelsful of earth onto the shiny-handled coffin. A gust of wind blew some damp earth into his face. He laid down the shovel, tried to brush the earth away with his sleeve, then went back to shoveling, with his eyes watering and his lips moving in a curse.

My father turned away when he saw the coffin disappear. Holding his head very low between his shoulders, he started to walk away, as if his presence were no longer necessary. I ran after him, but he was already out of sight among the monuments. I stopped to look at the photographs stuck into the tombstones. Some of them were old and discolored, others new. Concrete crosses alternated with slabs of polished white marble. Some distance away there were several miniature chapels which reminded me of my father's bird cages.

Carlo followed me, with his eyes on the ground. He too was looking at the graves, reading the names and dates on them. Together we walked toward the gate. Once we were outside he threw his arm around my shoulders. We stopped at a café to drink the usual hot chocolate. The woman from the floor above got a lift from the two other women who had come in the office car. We saw her drive away, waving her black-gloved hand.

"Are you cold?" Carlo asked me.

"No."

"Do you want to go home?"

"Not particularly."

"Where would you like to go?"

"I don't know. Let's just walk."

Carlo put his arm through mine and squeezed it. I was wondering whether Cesare knew of my mother's death and wished I could talk to him. We walked all over the city, from one street to another, stopping every now and then in front of a shop window, in order to rest rather than to look at the objects on display. Finally we bought some peanuts and sat down on a bench in the Villa Borghese. From behind the wall of the zoo we could hear the animals roaring.

"Have you ever been there?" asked Carlo, pointing to the gate.

"Once upon a time, when I was a very little girl."

"Then let's go have a look."

He bought the tickets and we went in. We didn't know which way to go first. Finally we went toward the monkeys, which were running up and down the artificial rocks, making angry noises. Every now and then they embraced and with a nervous movement of their hairy fingers picked the fleas off one another's backs. Carlo pointed to a little female with a bright red bottom, which was shelling nuts at an incredible speed. She shelled and smelled them and threw the shells away, all the while staring curiously at us out of her bleary eyes. I laughed, and Carlo squeezed my arm.

Next we stopped to see the giraffes, which were tearing leaves from the highest branches of the trees. A little farther on we found the dromedaries, sleepily ruminating. One of them, with a tuft of yellow hairs under his chin, was crouching on his front legs to masticate, and gazing at us. He was so near the fence that we could have touched him by reaching out a hand. When we started to go away he made a strange grimace. We turned to look back at him and found that we were still the objects of his stare. We threw peanuts to the elephants, which did not even turn around, and then we went into a hall where fish and snakes were on display.

The hall was empty. All the time we were in the zoo Carlo had not taken his eyes off me, following his usual tactics of watching and waiting. Now he propelled me into a corner across from an aquarium filled with transparent, black-striped fish. There he unbuttoned our two coats and glued our bodies together. He was keeping an eye, over my shoulder, on the door, while over his I saw the surface of the aquarium, with tiny bubbles bursting on the surface of the water. Someone was coming in, and so we drew apart and started toward the exit, at the opposite end of the hall.

"I'm tired," I said as soon as we were outside.

"Shall we go?"

"Yes. They're depressing, all those animals."

"They get used to being in captivity. You can get used to anything."

"No, not *any*thing."

"Perhaps you're right."

When I got home I helped my father to clear out my mother's room. He didn't want to see anything of hers around him.

"Take everything into your room," he told me, "including the wardrobe, with all the clothes in it. I don't need it here. If you like, I'll give you a hand."

"I'll see what I can use."

He had thrown open the window and was looking distractedly at the barracks across the way. When I opened the wardrobe I found it empty.

"The woman upstairs has taken everything away," I said.

My father wheeled around with a look of amazement. Then he laughed and laughed, until his laugh turned into a convulsive cough. It seemed as if a great weight had been removed from his chest.

"So much the better," he managed to say at last.

"But there were some wool scarfs, a blanket and a lot of shoes. The purple umbrella's gone, too."

"So much the better," he said, drying his eyes with his roughened hands. Then he went to fetch his one summer suit and hung it up in the empty wardrobe.

I carried away the few superfluous objects left in the room: a rag doll which my uncle had sent from America ten years before, a leather manicure case, three or four half-empty jars of cold cream and a box of ochre powder.

"Don't forget the dirty sheets," my father called after me.

[71]

Just then I remembered that in the wardrobe my mother had hidden an empty chocolate box containing two gold pins, wrapped in cotton, which had been given her by my grandmother. I went back to look for them, but without success.

"She's a thief," I said.

"Perhaps your mother sold them before she died," said my father, who was cleaning the mirror with an old stocking.

This was of course a possibility, and how could I accuse our neighbor? I went back to the kitchen, and soon after this my father went to take some papers to the insurance company. I lay down on my bed, throwing my coat over my cold feet. We'll have to be careful with our money, I thought to myself, if we want to live on what my mother has left us. I stared up at the network of tiny cracks on the ceiling. In the kitchen a tap was dripping, but for once there was no sound from the apartment next door. The telephone rang, and I rushed out into the hall.

"Is that you, Enrica?"

"Yes, Cesare."

"I'm sorry to hear the bad news."

There was an awkward silence. His voice was positively tender. "Why didn't you call before?" I wanted to ask.

"What did she die of?" he enquired.

"Cancer of the lungs."

He said nothing. Probably the mention of such a thing repelled him.

"I imagine you don't want to see me."

"I do, though."

"When can you come?"

"Whenever you say."

"How about tomorrow?"

"Is six o'clock all right?"

"Certainly."

11

I was ready by four o'clock, and at a loss as to how to spend the intervening time. I began looking through a picture magazine. My eyes fell on the pictures of an old couple who had committed suicide because they were so very poor. The two photographs were side by side, as I had seen some in the cemetery the day before. A pensioner and his wife. I stared at their faded faces without managing to feel any compassion. I was thirsty and went to the tap for a glass of water. A few minutes later I was thirsty again and squeezed some lemon juice into my mouth. Then I looked at myself in the mirror. I had washed my hair, and it tumbled in long, disorderly locks down over my cheeks. I gathered it all up into a knot and fastened it with a hairpin at the back of my neck. At a quarter to six I left the house. Just outside I ran into Carlo.

"How pretty you look! Where are you going?" he asked, barring the way.

"I have an engagement."

He scrutinized me in silence.

"Are you going to Cesare's?"

"Yes," I said, lowering my head. I was surprised that Carlo should know his name.

"Have a good time," he said brusquely and walked away.

I turned to look after him. He was walking with his head bent over, taking his usual light-footed, long strides. I pulled my coat around me and went in the direction of Cesare's house. I passed by the flower vendor's stall. On the front door of the house the blue ribbon, faded and dirty, was still hanging. I went up the stairs two at a time and arrived quite out of breath on the landing. I rang the bell, but nobody answered. I rang again, and after a few minutes Cesare's father came to the door.

"Well, my dear, come on in," he said, grasping my hand and blushing with pleasure.

"Where's Cesare?"

"He went out a short time ago."

"But he told me . . ."

"Oh, he'll be back soon. He probably went to a friend's house to study."

His gross, greedy face came close to mine and he breathed heavily as he made the gesture of helping me off with my coat. I stepped aside.

"For ages I've been hoping to have a word with you alone," he murmured into my ear.

And all of a sudden he drew me roughly to him, with his open lips searching for mine. I gave him a kick and with all the strength I could muster pushed him toward the wall. I caught a glimpse of his face, distorted with anger, and his arms groping for support. Already I was slipping out the door. I ran down the stairs and onto the street and didn't stop until I was some distance away. I walked blindly, without knowing where I was going, and the wind blew my skirt up over my knees. I went into a bar and ordered a drink, then I got on the first bus that came along. I sat in a corner beside a rattling window, which seemed as if with every bump it would shatter into a thousand pieces. Cradled by the motion of the bus I fell half asleep, until the laughing voice of the bus driver aroused me.

"Spending the night here, Signorina?" he asked.

I looked outside. It was quite dark and the bus had reached the end of the line. The seats were empty, the lights were turned off and the floor was covered with torn tickets.

"Are you ill?" said the bus driver, leaning over me.

"No, I'm not ill," I managed to say.

"We're a long distance from the center of town," he told me. "If you want to go back, take Number 7. It stops just around the corner on the other side of that apartment house."

I thanked him and got off. The wind was warmer now. The streetlamps had been lit, and I walked along in the track of my wavering shadow. There was a smell of cabbage and freshly baked bread in the air. I went around the corner, but I didn't wait for the Number 7 bus. I went straight down the street and then into another. I had never been in this section of the city, but I didn't care where I was anyhow. Probably it was in the southern outskirts of Rome, toward San Paolo. New apartment houses were lined up one beside the other on broad new streets, whose paving was already uneven and holey. The smell of fried fish, string beans, broccoli and coffee made me feel suddenly hungry. I was walking across a broad, empty square when an automobile drew up beside me and the door opened.

"Get in," said a masculine voice, and I obeyed.

The driver closed the door and held out a cigarette.

"Have a smoke?" he asked.

As soon as I had taken it he held out a lighter with his other hand. There was a heavy ring, with a coat-of-arms, on one finger.

"What's your name?" he enquired.

"Enrica."

"Let's go then, Enrica," he said.

The car got off to a silent start. It was a de luxe model with white leather upholstery and all sorts of shiny buttons on the dashboard. He drove with assurance, turning the steering wheel with only three fingers of one hand. Every now and then he looked at me and smiled. At a certain point he pushed one of the dashboard buttons.

"See if you can get some music," he said. "Turn that other knob."

I turned it until the arrow came to rest on a red line. There was a sudden explosion of music, and he made it even louder. I relaxed in the warmth of the heater, feeling as if I were in another world. He stepped on the accelerator, glided around a curve and threw on the brake. Then he stopped for a red light and started up again with a jolt. None of the other cars could keep up with his.

"Do you like to go fast?" he asked me.

"I love it."

"I'm taking you to my house. My family's gone off for a holiday at Cortina. It's fun, really, to be alone. I was wanting a girl just like you. Try to make yourself inconspicuous when you go in the house."

The car came to a sudden stop in front of a five- or six-story building with a shiny granite façade and a marble frame around the door. The liveried doorman came out of his lodge to see who was in the car.

"While I'm talking to him, you must slip in by the service entrance. Do you see that door over there? You'll find an elevator. Just take it to the top floor."

I nodded assent.

"Go! Run for it!"

I got into the dark elevator and pressed the button. I got out at the top floor, and a second later the elevator was sucked up by the darkness below. I didn't have long to wait before he opened the service door of his apartment and led me through a succession of rooms, switching on the lights along the way.

"What a gorgeous place!" I exclaimed.

He smiled and opened a compartment in the wall, lined

with mirrors and shelves containing bottles of every size and shape. He read the labels: "Cognac, Whisky, Pernod, Cherry Brandy . . . What'll you have?"

"Cherry Brandy."

He filled a liqueur glass and held it out to me. I emptied it with a couple of swallows. My mouth was filled with its sticky sweetness, and I made a face. He laughed.

"Take it easy! Have some more?"

"No, thanks."

He poured himself a glass of whisky and held it up to the light. "Nice color, isn't it?" And with a succession of tiny gulps he drank it down.

"Come here," he ordered, and I sat down at his side.

He pressed my head between his hands and examined it in the lamplight.

"How old are you?" he asked.

"Seventeen."

"You're a minor. . . . I really shouldn't . . . If I'm caught, you know, I'll go to jail. The trouble is that the younger they come the more I like them."

He toyed for a minute with his ring, shifting it from finger to finger. Then he got up and told me to follow. The bedroom was large and half empty. He lit a lamp on the bedside table, sat down on the silk bedcover and pulled me to him. He had blue eyes and a youthful smile, although his face was deeply wrinkled. He kissed me, first gently and then more roughly, pushing his tongue between my teeth. He took off my clothes and then, with a decisive gesture, tossed away his own. He had a delicate, sunburned body, a tuft of hair on his chest and bony shoulders. He lay on me lightly, taking care not to hurt. His skin smelled of soap and talcum powder. Little by little he heated up and flooded my belly. Both of us were dripping with perspiration.

"Did you like it?" he asked. Then without waiting for an answer he pulled back the curtain over one of the windows.

[77]

"Put out the light and come see," he said, with a voice that bespoke pride of ownership.

The window opened over the Villa Glori. Far below, on one side, the Tiber described a wide curve, with meadows on either bank; on the street in front of us cars noisily changed gears as they came up the hill. Near and far thousands of lights twinkled, looking like an amusement park.

"Gorgeous!" I exclaimed.

He turned around contentedly and kissed my eyes.

"Let's wash up," he said.

The bathroom tiles were white, with the design of a green sea horse. On the far wall there were two big black mirrors and on the floor a heavy pink wool mat, which tickled the soles of my feet. At one side there was a shelf groaning with bottles and flasks of perfume and lotions.

He turned on the shower and a stream of steaming hot water came out of the shiny metal outlet. I drew back for fear of being scalded, and he laughed. Then he took me into his arms and carried me under the water. With a big cake of yellow soap he rubbed my whole body. In turn, I soaped his back, causing him to laugh every time I came near his armpits. He wheeled around and put soap all over my face. I squealed and put my head under the steaming water. After he had turned it off we looked around us. The floor was flooded, the mat soaked, the soap had rolled into a corner and one of the bottles had fallen from the shelf and shattered into tiny pieces.

"A hell of a mess," I observed.

He drew me to him and kissed my neck.

"By the way, what's your name?" I asked him.

"Oh, I forgot to tell you. Giulio."

His cheeks were crimson and his eyes gleaming. He hopped around the flooded floor looking for a dry spot for his feet. I looked into the mirror. My hair lay in a wet tangle on my shoulders.

[78]

"Are you hungry?" he asked suddenly.

"Yes."

"So am I."

He wrapped a green towel around me and carried me back to the bedroom. After giving me a good rubdown he went to the bathroom and returned with a can of talcum powder. Throwing away the lid he sprayed me all over, as if I were a fillet of fish.

"Crazy!" I exclaimed.

"Just look! I'm going to fix myself up too." And he threw a fistful onto his shoulders.

He rubbed his body against mine, and the powder was like a veil between us.

"Did you say you were hungry?"

"Yes, I did."

"You'll have to wait a minute."

He drew me to him and roughly penetrated my body. When he was satisfied he withdrew and rolled over and over, drying the perspiration on the embroidered silk bedcover.

"I'm hungry myself," he announced, getting down on his knees to pull his slippers out from under the bed. "Do you know how to cook?" he added.

"Yes."

"Well, you don't have to. There must be plenty of stuff in tins."

I followed him into the kitchen. In the icebox there was a block of fresh butter and a bottle of milk. Giulio turned everything upside down in his search for some American tinned goods.

"Here is some shrimp, and here's smoked herring. As for this one, I can't make it out . . . it must be salmon. Which will you have?"

"I don't know."

"Shall we open all three of them?"

"Yes, let's."

After he had opened the tins I mixed the contents in a salad bowl. In a box he found a loaf of bread and cut it with a saw-toothed knife.

"Go to it," he said.

I spread butter on a slice of bread, which had a flavor of figs and licorice.

"Good?" he enquired, and I nodded, with my mouth stuffed, in reply.

After we had finished eating we went back to the bed and made love again, rolling over in one another's arms until we fell onto the carpet. We lay there, exhausted, side by side. Somewhere, in an empty room, a clock struck eight times. I thought I ought to call my father.

"I've got to go," I said.

"So have I. I'm supposed to be at an official dinner."

"How will you manage?"

"I'll have to eat a second meal, that's all. Luckily it's for late in the evening. Diplomats, you know. I'm a lawyer—did I tell you? A boring profession."

He kissed me on the cheek and started to get dressed. He threw a whole drawer full of shirts into the air in search of the one he wanted. After he had put it on he looked into the mirror and changed his mind. He threw it onto the floor and chose another that looked like its exact twin. As I pulled on my stockings I watched his frenzied movements out of the corner of one eye.

"I wish I knew what had happened to my cuff links," he grumbled, overturning a silver box. Then he remembered that he had left them in the bathroom. He put on a dark blue suit and knotted a blue polka-dot tie. While he stood in front of the mirror combing his hair he told me about the diplomats he was to see later in the evening.

"They're not to be trusted around the corner," he told me,

"but they happen to be useful. I have a marriage annulment on my hands which ought to yield me a mint of money. Meanwhile I'll have to talk horses and motorboats. I have a motorboat myself, but I'd rather take it out on the water than talk about it." He threw a last look into the mirror, smoothing his jacket over his hips.

"Are you ready?" he asked. "Come along. If you hurry I'll drive you home. Where do you live?"

"On the Via Moroni."

"Where's that?"

"Near Piazza Bologna."

"It's not on my way, but I'll take you there anyhow."

He kicked away the shirts, in which one of his feet had got entangled, and opened the door.

"No, this way. Down the service elevator, the same one that brought you up."

He propelled me through the kitchen and then shut the door behind me. I rode down in the service elevator and went out through a bare garden. When we were in the car Giulio turned on the radio and offered me a cigarette. He drove very fast, looking straight ahead of him and frowning.

"Where do I turn?"

"Farther on. I'll tell you when."

When I nodded he brought the car to a grinding halt in front of my door.

"Am I going to see you again?" he asked, taking his wallet out of his pocket and slipping a ten thousand lira note into my hand.

"I don't suppose so," I said feebly.

With nervous astonishment I crushed the banknote between my fingers. This was the first money I had ever earned.

"I rather like making love with you. How can I get hold of you another time?"

"This is my house. If you come by you can find me."

"I see. Very good. If you need money, remember my name's Giulio Guido. You'll find it in the telephone book."

"So long," I said, holding out my hand.

"So long."

As soon as I was out of the car, he drove off, leaving a blast of warm air from the muffler to strike me in the face.

12

In the kitchen I found my father dozing beside his bird cage. He started when I came in.

"Oh, it's you, is it?"

"Shall I fix you something to eat?" I asked him.

He shook his head.

"What would you say if we two went to have a bite outside?"

"I'm too tired. I want to get to sleep."

He looked at his roughened fingers. On the bottom of the cage his tools lay scattered: a gimlet, a hammer, a file, some pieces of metal and ends of string and a heap of tiny nails.

"I think I'll go to bed myself," he said, yawning.

The apartment was cold and smelled of faded flowers, those which had been standing in a vase ever since my mother's funeral. I threw open the window. The barracks courtyard was a square of light amid the dark houses. I thought back to the view from the house I had just left. How wonderful to look out at any hour of the day and see the Tiber! From my window I could see only a strip of sky that looked as if it were hung out on a clothesline and the all too familiar walls of the barracks.

My father had gone to bed when the telephone rang.

"Is that you, Enrica?"

"Yes. Who's this?"

"Cesare," he snorted. "Don't you know my voice?"

"Of course."

"Why didn't you show up today?"

"I did. Hasn't your father told you?"

"No."

"I came at six o'clock, but you weren't there."

"You might have waited."

I said nothing. Everything was so ridiculous.

"Where were you, anyhow? I called up three times."

"Oh, I was out on the town," I said, hoping that he would question me. But he was satisfied with my reply and did not investigate further.

"How about coming tomorrow?"

"Tomorrow I'm not free."

His voice sounded totally unreal. All I wanted to do was sleep.

"The day after, then."

"All right."

"Six o'clock?"

"All right."

"I'll be expecting you. Good night."

I put down the receiver and went to get undressed. My head itched and I scratched it. Some soap must have been left in my hair. I tried to summon up Giulio's laughing face. I remembered the individual features, but not the whole. A delicate, transparent nose, a narrow mouth with paradoxically full lips, crafty blue eyes, blue-veined white arms, wriggly feet, bony shoulders, and a tuft of graying hair on the chest. I spread the ten thousand lira note out on my pillow. That, too, was unreal. The longer I looked at it the more senseless it seemed. I folded it and stuffed it into the billfold that had belonged to my mother. Then I slipped in between the sheets and fell into a deep sleep.

The next day I went to school. I hadn't done my homework, and Old Lady Aiuti gave me a bawling out, while her daughter looked at me with scorn. She said nothing, but waved me away.

"If you go on like this you'll never get your diploma," said the mother, sitting down beside me and stroking my hair.

Gabriella was looking at Carlo, and Carlo was looking at me. Perhaps he knew about Giulio. I fancied I had seen him disappearing around the corner when Giulio brought me home the evening before. He barely nodded, and all during the lessons I felt his melancholy eyes staring at the back of my neck. I walked home alone, with the feeling that Carlo was following me.

At home I found my father working at his cage, with a bottle of wine standing on the floor beside him.

"How do you like this roof?" he asked, lifting up a tangle of wires with felt flowers stuck among them. "Something different," he went on, "like a pergola, don't you think?"

He stared at me out of gleaming eyes. For the first time I saw the resemblance between us. We had eyes of the same shape, and the same square nose. But he didn't really see me, any more than he had seen my mother before she died. From the way he batted his eyelids I guessed that he had been drinking. Yes, the bottle on the floor was half empty.

"Can I have a sip?" I said, picking it up and pouring some wine straight down my throat.

"That's no good for you," he said, snatching the bottle away and looking to see how much was left. Then he proceeded to gulp it down, his forehead furrowed with concentration. At the end he turned the bottle upside down, let the last drops trickle onto his hand and licked them up.

"My poor child!" he said all of a sudden, with a painful grimace, putting his arms around me and laying his head on my shoulder. I patted his scrawny neck and the white collar, blackened with fingerprints.

"Let me run you a hot bath," I said.

[85]

He got up and sighed.

"This cage is no good, you might just as well admit it. I make things that are of no use either to me or anyone else."

He leaned wearily against it. Then, with a visible effort, he picked up the hammer and went back to work.

"What if I were to make some changes, Enrica?" he said in a low voice. "Instead of the usual cupola I might top it with a pointed roof and a lacework balcony running around."

He was so absorbed by his project that he did not wait for an answer.

"Where are your insurance papers?" I asked.

He made a vague gesture in the direction of a chair where he had left his briefcase, filled with papers to be copied.

I sat down beside him and began, painstakingly, to make the copies. We worked, side by side, without speaking, until nearly three o'clock. Then I boiled some spaghetti and set out the cheese that was left over from the evening before.

After lunch I studied bookkeeping, and at six o'clock I went out for a breath of air. As I walked I thought of how much my father had changed in the last few days. He had gone back to drinking the way he used to before he was married. He forgot to wash himself or to come to the table. In fact he went to bed without even bothering to get undressed, and smelled stale and sweaty. He spent whole days over his bird cage, pausing only to tell me of some new idea for the roof or the interior decoration.

"Some day I'm going to get into one of these cages and never come out again," he said to me one evening, without raising his head.

13

I was late in getting to Cesare's on Tuesday. I only hoped that his father wasn't home and paused before ringing the bell. He was, though, and came to open the door, smiling as if nothing had ever happened, but avoiding my eyes. I went directly to Cesare's room, where I found him studying.

"It's hot in here," I said.

He closed his book and came to throw his arms around me.

"Listen," I began, "when I came here the other day your father . . ." And I started to push him away.

"Never mind," he interrupted, laying his finger on my lips. "I don't want to hear about it. Let's leave our parents outside this room. Can you promise me you won't think about your mother? It would only make both of us blue."

I leaned my head on his shoulder and let him impatiently undress me. I felt cold and had no urge to make love. He too seemed disappointed and turned his back. But he couldn't manage to go to sleep and finally turned around. With a smile as insincere as his father's he said: "Don't let's waste the day."

Gently he kissed my forehead. I recoiled when his hand began to run down my side. He took one of my nipples between his teeth and bit it. On the other side of the door I could hear his father's heavy breathing. Unconsciously I stiffened.

"What is it?" he asked.

"Your father."

"Just forget it. As far as we're concerned he doesn't exist. He has no right to."

I closed my eyes. Cesare's body clung to mine, the sheet grew warmer and warmer beneath us and the bed began creaking. Cesare cursed under his breath. I heard his father's footsteps retreat in the distance, and only then could I really let myself go. . . .

With our eyes shut we lay in one another's arms. His head was buried in the pillow and my lips clung to his shoulder. The telephone rang and Cesare answered it with his usual hypocritical voice.

"Was it Nini?" I asked when he had hung up.

"Yes. Why do you ask?"

"For no particular reason. When are you getting married?"

"Don't let's talk about that. It's too much of a bore."

I looked at his thick, half-closed lips, framed by the white pillow, at his face, with its weak features, framed by his silky blond hair.

"When will your exams be over?"

"Can't you think of *any*thing more fun to talk about?"

I shut up, not knowing what to say, and Cesare started to go after something to drink.

"What'll you have?" he asked me.

"Whatever's handy."

"Coca-cola?"

"Very good."

He slipped on his dressing gown and set off for the kitchen. I heard him talking to his father. Soon he came back with a couple of bottles. He hadn't thought of glasses, and so we drank straight out of them. After a few swallows I made a face and put my bottle down. I didn't care for that sugary, medicinal flavor. Cesare downed his with a few gulps. He wiped his mouth and gave a loud burp. I held out my practically untouched bottle.

"You don't like it, eh?" said Cesare.

"No, I don't."

"Why didn't you say so? . . . Oh well, I'll drink it myself."

He raised it to his lips and finished the drink with a single swallow. Then he said:

"You'd better be going. I've got to study."

I got up, collected my clothes from the floor and put them back on. Cesare was staring at his legs, as if he had never seen them before. There were circles around his eyes and his skin was drooping. He looked like an old man.

When I was ready he took me to the door and waited until I had started down the stairs before he closed it behind me. I went down the marble steps with the same feeling of disappointment as ever. I walked slowly back home. As I groped my way through the dark hall I quite suddenly thought of my mother's motionless, indifferent body, so closed within itself, on her deathbed. And then of the way I had seen her so often in the kitchen, standing over the gas stove with her legs spread far apart, her face swollen with fatigue and her house dress torn and faded.

I cooked something for my father and went off to bed. A short time later I woke up with a start, remembering that for several days now I had thought I might be pregnant. I got up and went out into the hall. After making sure that my father was asleep I dialed a telephone number.

"Cesare," I whispered into the mouthpiece.

"What is it?"

"I'm afraid I'm pregnant."

"You're nuts!" he shouted, with sudden alacrity. "How long have you had this idea?"

"For the last three weeks."

"Why didn't you say so before?"

"It just didn't occur to me."

"Little idiot! What are you going to do?"

He drummed the mouthpiece of the telephone with his fingernails as he reflected.

"First thing, take some laxative salts. Then soak yourself in a hot bath. Don't you know a doctor?"

"No."

"I'll talk to my father about it."

"No, not to your father."

"Why not?"

" 'As far as we're concerned he doesn't exist . . .' Don't you remember what you said when he was eavesdropping outside the door?"

"Yes, but I don't know what the hell to do."

"Perhaps Carlo can help me. He has an uncle who's a doctor."

"Who's Carlo?" he asked in a sleepily suspicious voice.

"A friend of mine."

He thought for a minute and then seemed to come around to this idea.

"Well, if you really think he can be of some use. . . . You know that just now I simply have to study. And then it's really your fault. If a woman doesn't watch out for herself, who's going to do it for her?"

"All right. I'll speak to Carlo."

"See what you can do. When it's time to pay, I'll take care of it, of course. I'm willing to take my share of the responsibility. . . . Listen, I'm dead tired, and tomorrow I have to go to the university. . . . Good night."

"So long." I went back to bed, but a short time later I got up again, thinking that I might as well get it over with as quickly as possible. I dialed Carlo's number, hoping that he would be the one to reply. I heard the click of the telephone and the tone of pleased surprise in his voice when he recognized mine.

"What's going on?" he asked. "Shall we have a date to-morrow?"

"That's not the question. I need you badly."

"What for?" he asked in alarm.

"I'm pregnant . . . by Cesare. Can you get your uncle to do something for me?"

He did not answer.

"Carlo!" I shouted.

"How long have you been this way?" He paused and then, with an audible effort, continued: "I'll help you, if you want. But my uncle's dead set against this type of operation, I know. He may tell me I can go to the devil."

"Then ask him for the name of somebody else. Giving a name doesn't involve him, does it? He knows what it's all about."

"Yes, but he's afraid. . . . Anyhow, I'll speak to him, per-haps tomorrow."

"Thank you."

"Good night."

I put down the receiver and went back to my room. I was terribly drowsy, but I couldn't seem to go to sleep. Perhaps the cold was keeping me awake. I curled up under the light, short blanket, with my knees under my chin. Finally I got out of bed and put on my wrapper. Then I spread my coat out over the foot of the bed and slipped in. I lay there with my eyes open and my hands folded between my thighs, staring into the darkness. I thought again of my mother and of myself as an old woman. I would be just like her, worn and dirty and indifferent to everything.

14

As soon as I got up I fixed myself a dose of laxative salts. It was very bitter, and tears of disgust came to my eyes as I drank it down. I found a bottle of wine in my father's room and took a couple of swallows to drive the bad taste away. The wine was red and slightly fizzy, with a flavor of grape seeds about it.

For several days now my father had been getting up early and going to the insurance company office. They had taken away the clerical work they had given him to do at home, because he brought it back in such sloppy condition, with all sorts of copying errors, not to mention spots of wine and grease. Now he had a job as a uniformed inter-office messenger, from seven in the morning until two in the afternoon, when he came home so tired that he didn't even want to work on his bird cage. He sat in front of his tools, dreaming up new techniques and stylistic innovations. Every now and then he licked a finger and ran it over one of the slender bars, staring adoringly at the elaborate curves of the metal structure. When he went out in the morning he left the bathroom in complete disorder. Once I found the pot in which he had been boiling some milk with the bottom reduced to a sort of silvery cream oozing over the lighted gas ring. For days on end the kitchen was filled with the sickening smell of melted aluminum.

After taking the salts I ran the bathtub full of water so hot that I had to ease myself into it little by little, holding on to both sides. Clouds of steam rose up from the bottom into my hair and eyes. At one point I thought I was going to faint and had to turn on the cold water and splash some over my face. Finally I got up, with my head as empty as if all the blood had been sucked down into my stomach. I sat down on a stool and threw a towel around my shoulders.

I thought of how my mother had waited in vain for years for a child, and when she had just about given up hope I had arrived on the scene. Perhaps she had tried to bring about an abortion. I imagined her in a tub of boiling water, with a white bath towel around her brown hair, her body already bearing the marks of both middle age and pregnancy. I could hear her calling for help from my father. At this time my father didn't make bird cages; he had a fairly good salary from the insurance company and took an interest in politics on the side. His face must have been not too unlike what it was now, but with livelier eyes and a less muddy skin. When my mother gave him the news he must have turned it into a joke and refused to believe it. Then, struck by the seriousness of her expression, he must have sat down on the edge of the steaming tub, run his hands through his hair and roared with laughter. "Just like Isaac!" he must have said, while my mother shrugged her shoulders. She was happy, now, over the prospect of having a baby, and smiled tenderly as she wiped herself dry.

I found myself smiling at my reflection in the mirror, with a strand of hair sticking to my cheek and my whole face reddened by the hot water. While I was getting dressed I turned on the radio in the kitchen and danced around the apartment with bare feet, until a chill traveled from my legs up into my spine. I put on my mother's gray bedroom slippers

[93]

and heated some coffee. It was wonderful to have a growing thing inside. Yes, being pregnant was out of this world.

When I came out of school Carlo overtook me.

"How are you?" he asked.

"Very well."

"You don't feel an urge to throw up?"

"No. I feel wonderful."

"I spoke to my uncle, but he wouldn't even listen. 'Think up something yourself,' he told me. 'I won't have anything to do with it.' I kept insisting, and finally he gave me the name of a medicine. But he said it was probably too late."

"I think I'll try it, though."

"Well, here's the name. I wrote it down on this scrap of paper. Do you want me to go to the pharmacy?"

"No, I'll go. Give it to me."

As he handed me the paper he glanced fearfully around him.

"What's worrying you?" I asked.

"Nothing. I'm on edge, that's all."

"Why? You're not involved."

"That's what you think. You don't know how deeply you concern me."

I crushed the paper between my fingers. I was thinking that Cesare ought to be happy to know that I was doing everything in my power to get rid of this troublesome child. I went into the first pharmacy we came to, leaving Carlo to wait for me outside. When I came out I had spent half of Giulio's ten thousand liras.

"Who's going to give me the shot?" I said to Carlo.

"I will."

"Do you know how?"

"Of course."

He followed my every gesture attentively, as if he were afraid of losing some subtlety of what I was trying to convey.

"My mother's syringe must be somewhere or other. Or else I can get Cesare to do it."

"He won't, I can tell you that," he said, with assurance, as if he knew Cesare better than I did.

"That's true. He's always having to study. And then he doesn't like responsibility."

"I'll come with you right now, if you like," said Carlo. "What time does your father get home?"

"At two."

"It's only half-past twelve. We have plenty of time. Shall I come on up?"

We quickened our steps in the direction of home and then went up the stairs two at a time, with Carlo leading the way.

I locked the front door of the apartment behind us, and then looked everywhere for my mother's syringe. Just as I was about ready to give up and go buy another I found it wrapped in a piece of newspaper, under a package of cotton in one corner of the bathroom. At once I boiled some water in which to disinfect it. Carlo stood in front of the window, not daring to move. His forehead was wrinkled, and he looked around him with his eyes popping with a mixture of curiosity and pain.

"The water's boiling," I told him. "Have you washed your hands?"

"No, I haven't," he said, spreading them out and examining them.

"Just push that door. It goes into the bathroom."

He walked toward it, as stiffly as a stick, and tried to open it the wrong way.

"There's no use pulling," I shouted after him. "Push!"

We both burst out laughing, and I almost dropped the pot of boiling water. Finally I regained my self-control and went, holding it gingerly, into my room.

"Do you know what's missing?" I said suddenly, after Carlo had taken the syringe into his hand. "Alcohol."

[95]

"Let's do without it," he said, trying to keep his hands from trembling.

"That's dangerous," I insisted, trying to think of something to take the alcohol's place.

"There's alcohol in wine, isn't there?"

"Yes, but not very much," Carlo said with a smile.

He had broken open the ampoule and was filling the syringe, drop by drop, while perspiration trickled down his cheeks and over his tightly closed lips.

"It would be better than nothing, though, wouldn't it?"

He agreed, and I went to get my father's bottle.

When I came back Carlo was standing very straight, with the syringe between his fingers and his eyes staring at its sharp needle.

"Ready?" he asked.

"Have a drink before you do it," I said, holding out the bottle and, with his eyes half closed, he took a long swallow.

"Feeling better?" I enquired.

"Much."

I lay down flat on my stomach and raised my skirt. Carlo stuck the needle into me so hard that I felt the impact even more than the puncture. Out of the corner of my eye I watched Carlo's contracted, intent face. Now that the needle was in he was afraid to hurt me by releasing the liquid.

"You're a funny one," I said.

"For God's sake, don't make me laugh," he grumbled. "Are you sure I'm not hurting you?"

"Of course not," I said.

When he finally pulled out the empty syringe we impulsively hugged one another.

"Thanks." I said.

Carlo held me tightly in his arms, trembling all over, and impelled me toward the bed.

"I don't really care for you," I whispered into his ear. But

I was aware of the warmth of his body against mine. He shook his head and held me even more tightly than before. We fell onto the bed and pulled the covers up over our heads.

15

Friday. The injection didn't seem to be producing any effect. I looked at my naked body in the mirror, trying to measure the curve of my belly. I looked at myself full face and in profile, without finding any real change. Cesare called me up every morning to hear how things were going.

"Anything new?" he asked shrilly.

"Not a thing."

Silence followed. I could hear a sigh at the other end of the wire, and then he went on talking in a hard, uninflected monotone. He couldn't see me because he had so much studying to do. Exams were drawing near and he hadn't done half the work. He was dead tired and extremely nervous because of the worry I had caused him.

"Nini has heard something about us, and she's making things tough for me," he said brusquely.

"What did you say?"

"I persuaded her that there was nothing to it. After that she recovered her peace of mind. But she telephones more often than she ever did before and she's got a way of dropping in without any warning. The little bitch!"

"Why are you marrying her?"

He fell silent and changed the subject. A few seconds later he said good-bye and hung up.

I was late to school and came into the classroom when the lesson was already underway. The first thing I saw was the obtuse face of Signorina Aiuti as it turned for a brief second toward the door, with her underlip mounting over the upper one in a motion which seemed to indicate that there was no use holding anything against us, no matter what we might do. After the interruption caused by my entrance she went on with what she was saying, leaning her head on her elbows and half closing her eyes. Carlo nodded in my direction and Gabriella stiffened.

No matter how hard I tried I couldn't follow what Signorina Aiuti was saying. The words came out of her mouth as monotonously and coldly as from a change-making machine and fell between the desks without leaving any trace behind them. Every now and then she paused, pursuing some line of thought all her own, and looked at us with an absent, glassy stare. Then she ran her hand through her hair, as if in an effort to wake herself up, and went on with the same monotonous explanation. I followed her with my eyes, and my ears were cradled by her voice, but my thoughts were far away, in Cesare's room, which I knew must be in its usual state of early-morning disorder. On the bed there was the imprint of his heavy body, and on the pillow that of his broad-beamed head. His pyjama trousers and overturned slippers lay scattered on the floor. The shutters were half open and a ray of dusty light cut the room in two. Cesare was sitting at his desk in a dressing gown half open over his chest, following with his eyes the motion of a winter fly, which flew over and over again through the ray of light from the window.

*

And yet the first time I ever saw him, on the beach at Maccarese, he seemed to be so lighthearted. After we had known each other for only a very short time he took me out in an old rowboat. When we were a certain distance away from the land he stopped rowing, kissed me and threw me into the cool, clear water. The salt pricked my eyes and nose, and I was laughing so hard that I swallowed bucketfuls of it. Cesare dove in after me. He threw his arms around my waist, and we embraced, treading water. He started to try to pull off my bathing suit, then changed his mind and swam away. He came back and splashed water in my face. We embraced again, breathlessly, because the waves were breaking against our faces.

"Shall we go back to the beach?" he said, in a voice that was muffled by the effort he was making to climb back into the boat.

After he was aboard he helped me to follow. We kissed, with the taste of the salt water still on our lips.

"Yes, let's go back," I said, and he squeezed my hands.

He sat at the oars and impatiently turned the bow toward the shore.

"How about over there?" he suggested, pointing to a part of the beach beyond the dunes, where underbrush and trees were growing.

I made no reply. Cesare stared at me intently but did not speak. Every now and then he shifted his gaze to look for a deserted landing place. Finally the keel scraped against the sand and he jumped into the shallow water.

"Come on!" he shouted.

I got out of the boat and helped him pull it up on the shore. Then he laid his hand on the back of my neck and I walked along, with lowered head, at his side. We went as far as the first underbrush, with the tall grass and thistles sticking into our legs, then turned inland and followed a path among the bushes. The blazing sun brought out the odor of the herbs, particularly the wild mint, and that of the dried cow dung along the way. The broom, burned to a crisp by the heat, crumbled under our feet. Suddenly, in the middle of a clearing, Cesare threw me onto the ground. He peeled off my bathing suit, which was wet and heavy with sand, and lay on top of me. He was my first man, and I got very little enjoyment out of it. I let myself go in his arms and cried, without even thinking. Cesare licked my tears away and tightened his arms about me. He was rough but tender, and afterwards he laid his cheek against my breast and talked about himself and me. I don't remember what he said, because I was half stunned and in pain. Finally my legs began to itch and I discovered that ants were crawling all over them.

"I want to go for a swim," I said.

We got back into our wet bathing suits and returned to the beach. The water was rougher now, but still crystal clear. We broke into a run and plunged in together.

After that we saw one another frequently, first at the shore and then at his house in the city. During the first months he was affectionate and thoughtful, but soon he became indifferent and one day we decided to break it off. We stayed apart for several weeks; then we met on the street and returned to making love regularly at his house, as before. To him it was just a matter of habit, but to me it meant a great deal more. Three years had gone by, and now I was faced with the fact that he meant to get married in the spring.

＊

Carlo's voice roused me from my reminiscences. The class was over, and Signorina Aiuti had left the room.

"A penny for your thoughts," said Carlo, brushing my hand with his fingers. Together we went toward the stairs. I was sleepy and had little wish to stay at school for another two hours. I gave voice to my impatience, while Carlo merely pressed his lips—with the shadow of incipient mustache

[101]

that overhung them—tightly together. When we finally left the school, at noon, it was with a feeling of liberation. The air was cold, but the sun was out and the clouds scudding overhead did not darken it. Gabriella tagged along beside us part of the way, complaining that her family kept her practically locked up in the house.

"My father doesn't know how to live," she complained, tossing her red hair over her shoulders. "He thinks we're still down in Apulia. 'If you're seen on the streets by yourself, what will people think?' That's what he's always saying. As if anyone here in Rome would pay any attention! Isn't it crazy?"

She was irritated by Carlo's silence and stared at him in the hope that he would notice the way her hair shone in the sun. But Carlo didn't seem to even see that she was there and finally she went her way, with a final flaunting of her hair.

"How goes it?" asked Carlo anxiously, as soon as she was out of hearing.

"Very well. I don't feel a thing."

"No nausea?"

"None at all."

"My uncle told me that you ought to have your urine analyzed if you want to be quite sure."

"So what must I do?"

He gave me a gesticulating explanation and then said that he would gladly take the bottle containing a sample of urine to the hospital if I didn't want to go myself.

"No, I'll do it," I told him.

"Then I'll go with you," he insisted.

We boarded a crowded tram, and Carlo gallantly saw to it that I wasn't pushed around by the other passengers. Standing like a ramrod he protected me with outstretched arms, as if I were a fragile and breakable object. He drew a sigh of relief when we arrived at our destination and I stooped to rub my foot where someone had stepped on it.

"I'd like to have a child by you," he said, lowering his head.

"I don't want a child by you or by anyone else," I retorted.

He did not speak for the rest of the way. In front of my house we shook hands and said good-bye.

16

Monday. In the afternoon I went to get the result of the urine analysis. It was positive. At the first bar I passed on the way home I called up Cesare.

"You little idiot!" he exclaimed when I told him. And he snorted into the telephone. "I'll give you the address of a friend of mine, Contessa Bardengo. She had the same thing happen to her and found a solution. I'll give her a call to tell her you're coming. Go there right away."

"And what shall I say?"

"Do you expect me to tell you? You ought to be able to figure it out for yourself. She's a woman of a certain age, and she's had quite a number of lovers, so you can be sure she won't start preaching to you. She's a bit odd, but lots of fun. Just now they say she's in love with someone twenty years younger than herself. Go along; I can't think of anything else for you to do. I'm pretty sure she'll give you a helping hand."

I took down the address and, with Cesare's irritated voice in my ear, went to find a bus going to the Via Cassia. The bus was half empty and rickety; when the driver threw on the brakes it jolted in such a way as to throw the passengers off balance. An old woman sitting just ahead of me made desperate efforts to hold on to her hat. From behind she looked very much like my mother. She had the same weary and anxious way of grasping at the nearest support. Now she held on to her hat as it slid down over her mass of dyed blond hair. I stared at her so hard that I forgot to get off at the right bus stop. In fact I went so far beyond my destination that I had to take another bus back in the opposite direction. After that I walked to the villa and waited for someone to open the gate. Soon I found myself going up a long pebbled driveway between rows of white rose bushes and violet cypress trees.

The villa itself was as white as whipped cream, with a fan-shaped stairway opening up in front of it, which led to a porch supported by marble columns. At the foot of the stairs there were two stone lions, with their mouths twisted into an ironical smile. A man in a sort of black uniform opened the door and looked at me with questioning eyes. I gave him my name, and he stepped aside with a bow. Then he shuffled ahead of me through two chilly, heavily curtained rooms, with glass cases along the walls. Finally we came to a circular room with a marble fireplace.

"Sit down," he said as he shuffled away.

I looked around. In the fireplace there was an artificial fire. Strips of plastic were lit up by a red light bulb which gave the illusion of a live flame. The mere sight of it made me feel suddenly chilly.

I was sitting on a small blue-and-white upholstered sofa, with gilded wooden arms, and sinking my feet into a thick rug with a Chinese peach-blossom design. Over my head there hung a glass chandelier with a multitude of iridescent pendants. Soon I heard clicking heels, and the Contessa Bardengo appeared before me. Her face was as powdered as a cake and wore a forced smile.

"Hello there, little girl," she said, holding out a heavily ringed hand. "We must have something to drink if we are to be friends, don't you agree?" And she opened a false bookcase, which seemed to contain leather-bound volumes but was in reality a bar.

"How about some brandy?" she said, pouring it into a balloon-shaped glass.

"Thank you," I said, stretching out my hand and gulping down a burning swallow.

As she stood before me I noticed that her body was much younger than her face. Her slender waist and rounded hips were circled by a band of black cloth with red lights playing upon it. As I examined her more closely I saw that she had beautiful black hair and that, behind the gold-rimmed glasses, her eyes were swollen, as if she had been crying. When she smiled her mouth was turned down at the sides like that of a mask, and there were deep furrows in her powdered cheeks.

"I'm pregnant," I said at last. "And Cesare said that you might help me."

"Cesare's a spoiled boy," she interrupted. "Didn't he tell you that he was my lover for some months a number of years ago?"

"No, he didn't."

"Well, there's no reason not to say so. But if you want my advice, I say you'd better drop him. He's a lazy, egotistical boy."

"But he's studying," I said in a low voice.

"Oh, he's studying, all right. But do you know how old he is? Twenty-eight. And I think he intends to go on studying indefinitely. He may get a degree some day, but I wouldn't say he was so very keen on study. Especially now that he's found a rich wife. You know about her, don't you?"

I bowed my head. To tell the truth, I rather liked the Contessa and I felt quite sure that her friendliness was disinterested.

"He told me all sorts of lies," she went on, pouring herself a second glass of brandy. "But what does that matter? I might have known he'd turn to me when there was some sort of trouble. That's just like him. He can't possibly face up to anything alone. He has a weakness for women and he's always getting himself into a mess. Then he doesn't want to take the consequences. His father's the same way. If you knew him better, you'd see what I mean."

"I know him well enough," I replied.

"Oh well, you're only a child, and of course you're in love with him. Nothing I can tell you will change your feelings. Don't protest. I know how it is. None of us learns from the experience of others. But one day the scales will fall from your eyes and you'll see him for the coward and opportunist he is."

I drank my brandy to the last drop while she was talking.

"Perhaps you love him just because he treats you so shabbily. It often happens that way. If you were indifferent he might care for you more. But what's the use of telling you these things? I'm in somewhat of the same fix myself. Did Cesare tell you? I was sure he would. But I'm not sorry, because now I can let down my hair and talk to you about it. . . . Old fool that I am, I sit here at home all day long, hoping that Remo will come see me! Even my own experience hasn't taught me anything, except to laugh at my folly."

She got up and poured herself another drink, offering more to me at the same time, which I waved away. Then she sat down again beside me, crossing her long legs which were encased in net stockings.

"Remo's eighteen years old!" she exclaimed. "Just your age —or am I mistaken?"

"I'm seventeen."

"I could be his mother and yet I'm crazy about him. I even have a weakness for his stupid friends and his money-loving family, which winks at what's going on because I'm a rich woman. I don't know why he ever went for me at all. Probably because it was to his advantage, and yet there are times when I fancy he does love me a little. Actually, I don't understand him. He lies so smoothly that I can't be angry. Sometimes he's affectionate and thoughtful; at others he's hard as a stone. Mind you, he doesn't ask me for money. I'm the one to offer it, perhaps in the hope of putting him under an obligation. . . . Just look, every time I talk about him my hands start sweating. There are days when I'd like to kill him to put an end to my torture. But probably this torture is part of my love. I see the situation quite clearly, but I can't seem to get away from my feelings. His looks are commonplace; he has a weak face, a skin that's as milky-white as that of a baby and teeth as sharp as a dog's. But I love everything about him, even his faults; perhaps I love them best of all: his vanity, indifference and selfishness, his dirty nails, his hairy back, his greasy hair and the shamelessly greedy expression on his stupid face."

She gave a deep sigh, took another sip from her glass and went on, tapping her rings against the rim.

"What do you suppose I do all day long? I just sit around and wait for him to ring or call. When I can't stand it any longer, I lie on my bed with a bottle of brandy and a pile of magazines and sometimes, for a few minutes, I manage to forget him. Alcohol clouds my memory. I feel like a cat, half asleep and purring, while she waits for a mouse to come out of its hole. Yet when he telephones I have nothing to say; I'm afraid of boring or irritating him. I wait nervously for him to say something agreeable or to sweeten his tone of voice, but that doesn't happen very often. Usually he tells me a pack of lies about how he's been spending the day; he takes pleasure in the most unlikely and absurd inventions. For the sake of my peace of mind I try to believe him. But as soon as evening comes I get into my car and stalk them. I try to find out from his friends where he has gone, and of course they laugh at me behind my back. But I've gone beyond the point of caring what people say. Once upon a time it mattered, let me tell you. I was always asking people to my house; every evening I gave a cocktail or dinner party. I went to great pains over my clothes and drove everywhere in my car. Now all that sort of thing disgusts me—the masculine fashion plates and their best-dressed wives and their drawing room gossip. Once upon a time this fireplace was always blazing. Beside it there was a pile of wood that went all the way up to the ceiling. I tossed great logs onto the fire, mixed drinks and put records on the phonograph; in short, I was the perfect hostess. Remo was the one that insisted upon having an artificial fire. I know it's vulgar and horrible, but I like it that way because he bought and arranged it."

She stared tenderly at the painted logs, while her eyelids swelled with tears.

"And when my husband was alive . . ." she continued, wiping the tears away with the back or her hand, ". . . there was a man who knew how to have a good time! He was always pursuing some new idea or some new woman." She laughed and took off her glasses in order to wipe them on the hem of her slip. "Until one day he ran away to Switzerland with a sixteen-year-old girl and nobody ever saw him again. But he was on the level; he never asked me for a penny and I don't know how he manages to support her. This house was left me by my father who—I'm sure Cesare must have told you—was in the fur business and made a fortune during the years between the two wars. It's ugly, of course, from an architectural point of view. Every time I look at those lions I imagine that they're laughing at me, and at my father, who brought them, as a bargain, all the way from a village in Umbria. You saw them, didn't you? They're comical, you must admit. Remo's always laughing at them too. He says that their mouths are like mailboxes, and he's always sticking his hand inside to see if they have teeth. Oh well, he's only a child; as I said before, he's not much older than you. You ought to see the way he dresses. He's got an idea that he wants to be a film actor, and he goes around in leather jackets and dungarees and cowboy boots, which cause people to turn around and stare. But I'm not ashamed to be seen with him; in fact, I'm actually proud because in his way he's a very handsome fellow. He has the same slanting, intelligent eyes as Sophia Loren, not to mention a bold, broad forehead. What a boy he is! You really ought to see him."

She had put down her glass and was toying with her pearl necklace. The pearls were as tiny as grape seeds and absolutely snow-white in color.

"I must be boring you to death," she said, turning to look at me.

I shook my head.

"Of course I am. You came here for a purpose of your own, not simply to listen to me talking. Of course I'll be glad to help you. I can give you the address of a first-class midwife. At first she's bound to raise objections, but just tell her that I sent you. Don't pay her more than twenty thousand liras, do you understand? She's greedy as a pig and works overtime in order to make money for her stupid, capricious daughter. But at heart she's a good woman and she knows her business. Here's her address." And she held out a cigarette box on which she had scribbled with her eyebrow pencil. "Right underneath is the telephone number."

I slipped the box into my handbag.

"Thank you, Contessa," I murmured.

"I'm no contessa," she objected. "My father bought the title, and up to a short time ago it was important to me as a part of my social life. But now I hate it. I'd gladly give away both title and money in return for being ten years younger, so that I wouldn't have to feel so ashamed when Remo looks at me."

She got up, adjusting her glasses on her nose. She looked into the opaque mirror hanging near the door and then led me across the threshold. I stumbled after her across the thick rug. The high frescoed ceiling hung over my head like the vault of a church, filled with echoes and cobwebs.

"Good luck, Enrica," she said, grasping my hands.

"Thank you."

I looked for the last time into the tear-swollen eyes behind her gold-rimmed glasses and turned around to go down the stairs. At the bottom I stopped to look at the lions, which crouched on green-veined marble pedestals. There were painstakingly sculptured curly manes behind their ears, and their curved mouths were toothless. I walked back down the driveway in the twilight, between the cypress trees and the rose bushes. Then I retraced my steps along the street to the bus stop at the corner.

17

That evening I called the midwife. She maintained a guarded and suspicious attitude and asked me all sort of questions, but finally she was persuaded to set an hour when I could come to see her on the following Thursday.

I went back to the kitchen to cook supper. My father was kneeling on the floor with his trouser legs rolled up. His hands were sticky with glue and he was filing some tiny wooden bars before fitting them into position. A bottle of wine stood on the floor beside him; every now and then he mechanically raised it to his lips, without taking his eyes from the cage. He had put the top together and taken it apart several times without satisfaction. He would break a wire with the pincers and then weld it together with a new blowtorch of which he was very proud. He had brought it back to the house rolled up in a newspaper and showed it to me as if it were his dearest treasure.

"Do you like it?" he had asked.

Then, without waiting for a reply, he kissed me on the cheek, took off his jacket and started to work.

Sometimes he forgot to turn it off, and the red-hot torch caused some of the tiles of the kitchen floor to crumble. Two fingers of his left hand were burned, and every now and then they were so painful that he had to lick them.

"How much did that gadget cost?" I asked him now, with some irritation.

"Plenty," he replied.

"We could have eaten a good bit of meat for that money," I said resentfully.

"You talk like your mother," he said, reaching for the wine.

"Or you might have bought some decent shirts," I went on. "The three that you own are in shreds. Every time I wash them I'm afraid they'll fall apart."

He shrugged his shoulders and turned on the torch, proceeding almost at once to scorch his fingernails.

As I stood over the kitchen stove I heard the monotonous roar of the blowtorch flame.

"Supper's ready," I called out at last.

I was dead tired. The painted, sorrowful face of Contessa Bardengo was dancing before me. I could see her tears, enlarged by the lenses of her glasses, trickling down from under her reddened eyelids. My head ached, and I shut my own eyes. The coffee, ready on the stove, had a sickly sweet smell. I put two bowls of rice on the table and sprinkled them with cheese. I rinsed two glasses for the wine and took knives, forks and spoons out of the drawer.

My father sat down at the table, his fingers still smeared with glue. With his head between his shoulders he stirred the cheese into the rice.

"You didn't wash your hands," I said disgustedly.

He examined them, shook his head and started to eat, without raising his elbow from the table. I lowered my eyes and made an effort to force down some of the rice. But I had no appetite. My joints ached, and I had a feeling of nausea in the pit of my stomach. My father alternated a forkful of rice with a sip of wine, wiping his lips with the back of his hand.

"Couldn't you use your napkin?" I asked him.

He raised his eyes in astonishment and went on eating,

holding his head even lower than before, as if he wanted to hide it between his narrow shoulders.

"Would you like an egg?" I asked him.

He shook his head.

"You ought to eat more," I told him.

"No," he said brusquely. "Just give me an apple."

I took away the bowl and set the fruit dish, containing three yellow apples, in front of him. He washed one off and tried to polish it with his sticky fingers. Then he started to bite into it but gave up almost immediately because of his bad teeth and threw it away.

"Damn it! I'll have to get dentures," he grumbled.

Meanwhile the apple, having bounced against the wall, rolled across the floor and came to rest under the sink. My father gave it an angry look. Then he rose from his seat, hiking up his baggy trousers.

"A cup of coffee," he said curtly, sucking his teeth and going back to his blowtorch.

I heated the coffee and poured it into the blue Canton china cup which my mother had inherited from my grandmother. Then I put the cup on its saucer and handed it to him. He drank down the coffee with a gurgle of pleasure.

"Very good," he said, laying the cup and saucer down at his feet.

When I leaned over to pick it up I felt as if I were losing my balance. My head was heavy, and once more the smell of the coffee made me feel sick. I opened the window and stuck out my head, but there was the dense heat of the sirocco in the air. I took a deep breath and thought that I really ought to call Carlo. He was sure to be worried about me. But I didn't want to speak to him. Strangely enough, I had no urge to call Cesare either. What could I say?

I shut the window and went to wash the dishes. The neighbors' television was blaring, and from time to time an unusually loud burst of music made me shudder. In order to fight off the obsessive tune I hummed a song my mother had taught me.

"I'm going to bed," I shouted out when the dishes were done.

My father nodded absent-mindedly, grasping the blow-torch as if it were a dagger and staring at the cage. I shut the door behind me, undressed more quickly than usual and stretched out between the cool sheets in the darkness. As soon as I laid my head on the pillow I fell into a deep sleep.

18

Thursday. The sky was full of smoky gray clouds, whose drifting shadows alternately hid and disclosed the sun. The hot sirocco was blowing. I woke up with a headache and aching limbs, as if I had spent the whole night on my feet. Carlo knew about my appointment with the midwife and called me the evening before to say that he wanted to lend me his moral support.

"You can't go alone," he insisted. "I'm going with you."

"But I want to go alone."

"I'm coming, anyhow."

"Please don't," I said feebly, knowing that nothing would deter him.

Cesare had telephoned on Tuesday to find out whether I had gone to see Contessa Bardengo. He was glad to hear that all was well.

"So you're going to the midwife," he said. "When?"

"Thursday."

"I'll pay the bill; you can count on that."

"Very good."

"Do you think it's going to hurt?"

"I don't know."

"I'll be thinking of you that afternoon. What time is your appointment?"

"Half-past three."

"That's when I'll think of you, then. If I didn't have so much work to do I'd come along."

"Don't worry."

"Well then, good luck!"

"Thanks."

"Don't go blabbing to everyone you meet. I mean don't mention my name."

"Don't worry about that, either."

"Who's worried? You never can tell, that's all. I don't want to be mixed up in anything shady."

"I'm not blabbing."

"Good for you. I'm going to give you a present that will make you forget all your troubles."

"Thanks."

"Where did you get that flat voice? You sound as if you didn't love me any more. Do you?"

I laughed hysterically.

"What is there to laugh about?"

"Nothing."

"Well, so long."

I heard the click which meant that he had hung up. With my ear glued to the receiver I listened to the rustling silence. I had spent two tiresome days at home, simply because I didn't have the nerve to go to school. At one point I went out of the house, because I couldn't stand looking any longer at my father, who as usual was busy with his bird cage. I walked distractedly, looking at the passers-by and the shop windows, until I found myself in front of Cesare's door and realized how much I wanted to see him.

I walked up and down, hoping that he might come along, until finally I made up my mind to go home, with a feeling of nausea in my stomach.

And so, at last, Thursday came around, and I only wished that its dragging hours would go by. I wasn't able to eat a thing for lunch, and by a quarter to three I was out on the street. My father had wolfed down some spaghetti, without even stopping to drink any wine. Then he threw himself, in his clothes and shoes, on his bed and in a few minutes he was snoring. I walked along the Via Nomentana, under the trees, with cars and buses passing me noisily by. Before turning into the Viale Regina Margherita, I stopped at a café for a drink of water. The smell of coffee inside disgusted me. When I reached the house I made sure that it was the right number and climbed the stairs all the way to the top floor. I rang the bell, and a girl my own age came to answer. She was wearing tight black slacks; her blond hair fell over her shoulders and her lipstick was pale pink.

"Oh, it's you, is it?" she said, scanning me from head to toe and then shouting down the hall: "Mother, she's here!"

Out of the darkness, redolent of cooking grease, came a little woman, with her mouth full of food and a napkin in one hand.

"I'm sorry, I was eating," she said, making an effort to swallow what was in her mouth. "I have so much to do that I never find time to sit down to a proper lunch." And she added, to her daughter: "Take her in there to wait."

The girl opened a glass door which led into a rectangular room. Against the far wall there was an operating table with tubular aluminum legs and a piece of white oilcloth thrown over it. A flowered curtain masked the window, and under the sill, in a white enamel cabinet, there were some surgical instruments, two upturned basins and a pile of absorbent gauze.

"Make yourself comfortable. I'll be with you in a minute," the midwife called out.

I sat down on the edge of the table. In one corner I saw an electric heater, apparently a recent acquisition, since on it there was a factory tag, slightly yellowed by the heat.

The girl was talking on the telephone. I heard her say that

she couldn't go out for another half hour, because she was busy. Whoever was on the other end of the wire insisted, and with a snort she hung up the receiver. A few minutes later I heard her singing in another room.

"Hurry up, Mother," she called out in a shrill, bossy voice. "I want to go out."

"Just a minute," her mother answered calmly. "I have to sterilize my instruments."

Shortly after this she came in and handed me a pill.

"Take this," she said; "it's a sedative." And she shouted to her daughter: "Patrizia, bring a glass of water."

Patrizia stared at me as I struggled to swallow the big green pill.

"Did you get it down?" she asked, batting her long eyelashes inquisitively. And when I nodded she went out, slamming the door.

Soon her mother, who had disappeared, came back in, with her sleeves rolled up, carrying a basin of hot water.

"Take off your coat and your panties," she ordered.

I threw my coat onto the table. Then, leaning against the wall, I raised my skirt and slid down my panties. She laid down the basin and put on a white smock and a pair of transparent rubber gloves.

"Lie down."

I looked at her nervous hands, encased in the overly large gloves, her hard, deeply wrinkled, expressionless face and her white hair, gathered up in a colorless net.

The next thing I knew a long instrument was inside of me. But the pill had made me sleepy and at first I felt nothing. Suddenly the instrument began to move, jerkily, and I was shot through by a pain as intense as that of an electric shock, which caused my teeth to chatter. Everything seemed to be falling apart, and I cried aloud in my agony.

"For God's sake, shut up! If the neighbors hear, I'll be in real trouble. Shut up, I tell you!"

[119]

I raised my hand to my mouth and bit it. The metal circle contracted and expanded, leaving me in a state of utter exhaustion.

"It's almost over," she told me.

I held my breath, while my scalp, neck and armpits dripped with perspiration.

"That's all," she said, spiriting away the basin before I could see what was in it. "Lie there quietly for a few minutes, and then you can go home."

I lay back with a sensation of well-being now that the pain had subsided.

The midwife came back with another pill and another glass of water. She watched my attempt to swallow, and in her indifferent eyes I saw a gleam of understanding and compassion. She smiled, revealing her yellowed teeth, and ran her fingers through my damp hair.

"I'll bring you the twenty thousand liras within a few days," I told her.

"Very good," she said, reassuming her indifferent air.

Then her daughter came in, bringing me a cup of hot milk.

"Thanks," I said, gulping it down, unaware of the taste but with my throat burning.

They left me there, under a blanket, for a good half hour. The midwife turned on the heater, and around the central disk I saw the wires begin to glow. I heard the daughter go from one room to another, first in bedroom slippers and then in high heels, until she left the apartment, calling out goodbye.

"It's time for you to go," said the midwife, helping me to my feet. She had taken off the white smock, and was fastening up her skirt with a big pin. By way of farewell she held out a soapy hand.

"You may have some pain during the night," she explained. "Take a sleeping pill and stay calm. You'll feel better tomorrow. Be sure to let me hear from you before Sunday, or

[120]

else I'll have to get after Contessa Bardengo. It's only because of her recommendation that I'm charging you so little."

She closed the door behind me, and I went slowly down the stairs, hanging on to the banister. Just outside I found Carlo waiting for me, standing against the wall. He moved forward with a look of concern.

"How are you?" he said, grasping my arm.

"Quite all right."

"Did it hurt?"

"Not much, really."

"Do you want something to eat or drink, or would you rather go home?"

"I'd rather go home."

"Good," he said, holding me up as if I were incapable of walking alone.

"Perhaps we should take a taxi," he suggested.

"I'm quite all right, I told you. There's no reason not to walk."

"Yes, there is," he retorted, pushing me into a black-and-green taxi which was waiting at the street corner.

19

As I came into the apartment I imagined I heard my mother complaining to my father in her usual way. I stopped short for a moment before going through the kitchen door and discovering that it was only the radio. Abruptly I turned it off. My father raised his head and looked at me out of unsteady, gleaming eyes. Behind the bird cage I caught sight of a bottle of wine.

"I'll wager you've spent your whole week's salary," I said. "And mother's savings will soon be gone too."

"I make quite enough to cover expenses," he retorted. "As long as I'm around you'll have food to eat and a roof over your head."

"You're drunk."

"What's that?" he protested indignantly. "I don't get drunk. I drink only in order to keep warm. Right now I must finish this cage and sell it. I want to make something extra and buy you a new coat. I'll not have you going around like a beggar. You need some shoes, too. This is the biggest cage I've ever built, big enough to hold twenty parrots, or even an eagle. I have an idea who'll buy it. The zoo! What do you think of that? I might even get an order for a whole set of cages in which to house their tropical birds. In that case I could leave the insurance company and get rich selling cages. What do you say?"

I didn't answer. It surprised me that I didn't feel any pain. The next thing to do was to make some soup. I started to boil some onions and potatoes, together with a piece of horse meat, which had a moldy smell because it had been sitting around for days wrapped up in a piece of paper. With the meat I threw in a pinch of salt and a teaspoonful of vinegar. As I was cutting a potato in two I thought about Cesare. Just then the telephone rang and, drying my hands on my skirt, I ran to answer.

"How did it go?" he asked hurriedly as soon as he heard my voice.

"All right."

He sighed with relief.

"No more trouble, then, is that it? You're just the way you were before."

"Yes."

"I'm glad. I was so afraid you were suffering that I couldn't put my mind on my work."

"When shall I see you?"

"Nini is always on my tail these days. She's a pest, I can tell you. With one excuse or another she's sure to be hanging around. Besides, you shouldn't make love in your present condition. After all, you've had an operation."

"But when am I going to see you?"

"I don't know. We'll think about that ten days from now. Meanwhile take it easy, eat and sleep and look after yourself."

"Do you mind if I call you up tomorrow?"

"Not tomorrow. I'm going to study over at a friend's house the whole day. You can try me the day after."

I hung up, and got back to the kitchen just in time to rescue the soup from boiling over. I threw in some alphabet noodles, and turned down the gas. Then I went to take off my shoes and ripped stockings, to lay my underwear across the back of the chair and put on my mother's house dress, whose neckline was stained with perspiration. In the bathroom I bathed my hot face in cold water. Looking into the mirror I saw my mother, with heavy dark lines under her eyes and a tired, flaccid body. My gestures were exactly like hers. When I returned to the kitchen my father started as if he were seeing his wife, and reached for the wine bottle.

"Supper's ready," I said.

Gusts of cold air blew in upon my legs through the cracks at the edge of the window frame. We ate in silence, listening to the faraway sound of the shrill bus brakes on the street outside. Our neighbors must have been out, for the TV was silent. The wind caused the windowpane to rattle. When I got up to take away my father's plate he grasped my hand.

"Poor little girl," he murmured.

"What's the matter?" I asked with annoyance. I wished I could obliterate him from my sight and go to bed.

"Poor little girl," he repeated, dropping my hand in order to reach out for the wine.

"You're drunk," I told him.

He raised the bottle to his lips and drank, without stopping to breathe, as if he were drinking water. Then he took a crumpled handkerchief out of his trouser pocket and wiped his mouth and forehead.

"That's my weak point," he said. There was a laughing expression in his eyes and his face was that of an old monkey.

"I'm going to bed," I said.

"This early?"

"I'm half asleep."

He came over as if to give me a hug, then changed his mind and waved his hand.

My room was cold and stuffy. I threw open the window and leaned out for a breath of fresh night air. Then I closed it and slipped in between the sheets, throwing my coat and dressing gown over the foot of the bed. The cold prevented me from going to sleep, and finally I summoned up the energy to get up and put on a pair of wool socks. Curled up in my bed I listened to some women's voices in the courtyard and then to the whirring of a motorcycle engine which wouldn't start. Little by little I began to feel warm. I stretched out my legs and half dozed off. I was awake enough to hear the sounds around me, but every now and then I fell asleep, and dreams poured through my mind as tempestuously as the waters of a mountain stream.

I saw myself in the rowboat with Cesare. Waves rippled under the keel, and the surrounding air was bright and warm. Cesare was licking the salt off my eyelids. The sun was devouringly hot. All of a sudden I found myself in the shade of the inside of Cesare's mouth, while his eyes searched for me in vain. I made myself small, very small, and he swallowed me as if I were a eucharistic wafer. Something was burning inside my stomach. Cesare stuck in his hand and pulled out a wad of cotton. The midwife told me that it was all over, but I still had the same burning sensation inside. I said something to Cesare about it, and he hugged me tight. His blond hair fell suffocatingly over me. The thing inside my stomach became increasingly alive and painful. I complained to Cesare and he told me to go see Contessa Bardengo. But she had lost her glasses and didn't know who I was. A boy wearing a black leather jacket laughed in my face. I gulped down a swallow of brandy, and it burned my throat. Cesare had disappeared without leaving any trace behind him. I was alone in the boat, with the sun blazing inside my stomach. At this point I suddenly awoke, with a sharp pain. I got up, switched on the light and drank some water. My father must have already gone to bed, for the whole apartment was dark.

I groped my way to the bathroom, and holding my hand over my forehead I leaned over the toilet. I vomited abundantly. Then I stood in the dark, reeling with dizziness and powerless to move. Finally I managed to go over to the basin, turn on the water and douse my head, but still I didn't feel any better. I went back to my room and lay down on the bed with my hand over my mouth. The pain rose in a crescendo like that of a wave, after which it subsided, draining all my strength from me. Tremblingly I got up again, to look for a tranquillizer. In the bathroom I found some belladonna and poured a few drops into a glass of water. I lay down again on my bed, pressing my hands to my stomach and shivering all over. "You jackass!" I said to myself. "That midwife's left you stuck with an infection." But little by little the pain subsided, and I fell once more into a state of dozing. Suddenly I opened my eyes and saw my father, in his pyjamas, standing sleepily before me.

"What's the matter?" I asked.

"You were moaning. Are you sick now, like your mother?"

Outside everything was quiet. It must have been three or four o'clock in the morning. I heard a tap dripping in the kitchen.

"Is it serious?" my father asked, bending anxiously over me.

"No," I said, turning toward the wall.

"I've never been a real father to you," he said in his usual calm manner.

"Just let me go to sleep, Father."

"No. There's something I must say. You've been unlucky. Your mother and I conceived you without love. I've never given a hang about you. The only things I've ever cared for have been my little hobbies. I'm absolutely no good. I'm neither the artist I wanted to be nor the father I should have been."

He talked in a low, toneless voice, as if he didn't care whether or not I was listening. I wanted to tell him to go back to bed, but I lay stiffly against the wall, with my hands pressing my stomach and a bitter taste in my mouth.

My father stood staring at me. Perhaps he was waiting for me to go back to sleep. Suddenly I heard his bare feet shuffle across the floor and his face brush my hair. He kissed my cheek, leaving a strong odor of wine in my nostrils.

"Good night, little girl," he said, pulling the bedcovers over me and shuffling away.

20

I spent several days in bed, getting up only to answer the telephone, in the hope that Cesare might be the one to call. Carlo came to see me every afternoon. He sat on a chair at the foot of the bed, with his hands pressed between his thighs, and stared at me. Sometimes he brought a magazine.

My father got up a half hour earlier than usual in order to make me a cup of hot milk. He was late getting off to the office and dashed out with his trousers unzipped, his tie in his hand and the smell of wine on his breath. At about two o'clock he came home, bored and tired, and walked with dragging feet into my room.

"How are you?" he said.

"Better."

"Are you hungry?"

"Not really."

"I bought some sausages. Is that all right?"

And he showed me the wax-paper package he was carrying under his arm. I heard him move awkwardly about the kitchen, upsetting pots and pans and spilling water. Half an hour later he came back to my room carrying a tray on which he had put the pan in which he had cooked the sausages and eggs, and a heel of bread.

"Delicious," I said, and he peered at me as if he didn't believe what I was saying.

"Would you like some wine?" he asked, but then he forgot to go get it.

In the afternoon he worked at his cage. When Carlo came he usually went out to a tavern and came back drunk.

One morning the landlord rang the bell and I went in my wrapper to answer. He was a thin man with a yellowish mustache and a mournful expression.

"I came for the rent," he said. "You owe me for four months. Your father said he'd pay up after the funeral. I didn't want to intrude upon your sorrow. . . ."

He paused, and held one hand in front of his mouth in embarrassment. At the same time he scrutinized the dark, empty rooms behind me.

"I'll speak to my father about it when he comes home," I told him.

"You needn't bother. I met him on the stairs earlier this morning. But to tell the truth—and I don't want to offend you—I had a feeling he wasn't himself. I realize that grief for the loss of a dear one may incline a man to certain weaknesses, especially one who, like your good father, hasn't a job of the kind he deserves."

He looked down at his highly polished black shoes, coughed two or three times and shifted his weight from one leg to the other. Suddenly he raised his small, glittering eyes and said abruptly that if the back rent wasn't paid within three weeks he would put us out of the apartment.

"It's not just meanness, Signorina, I'm sure you understand that," he said in a ruefully subdued voice. "I live off the rent from this house, and if a tenant doesn't pay I have to borrow money to meet my bills. I haven't enough leeway to let things go."

He pulled a freshly ironed black-bordered handkerchief

[129]

out of his pocket, delicately wiped his nose and smiled, disclosing two rows of tiny, very straight teeth.

"Will you have a cup of coffee?" I asked, pointing to the kitchen.

"No, no," he said hurriedly, as if he were afraid of compromising himself.

"Well, what am I to do about the rent?" I enquired.

"Girls can have a great influence over their fathers, and you're no longer a baby. If your father were to give up certain rather expensive . . . er . . . bad habits, he could apply himself more clearheadedly to the solution of the problem. You must make him feel aware of his responsibilities. I know that he doesn't make much money. But if he saved up what he spends on alcohol and also—if I may say so—on those things—I don't know what to call them—that he's always building . . ."

"Cages . . ."

"Of course, cages . . . I mean if he were to take up some better paid kind of work . . . It's not up to me to interfere or give unsolicited advice. But it's better that I should talk frankly than get rough. I truly don't want to put you out. You've been here for ten years and your parents have always managed, somehow, to pay the rent. Now I find myself in a delicate situation. I have to go against my own better instincts because I have a duty toward my own family. . . ."

I cut him short, saying that I was tired and would have to think it over. Then I said good-bye and shut the door in his face. I heard him go light-footedly down the stairs, coughing as he went. My feet were freezing cold and I hurried back to bed. When my father came home I immediately told him the story.

"I don't see why the stupid fool had to come to you," he said with annoyance.

"We have three weeks before he throws us out."

"Don't worry. I'll find the money."

"How?"

"I have a job, don't I? I'll ask for an advance on my salary. And then I may very well finish and sell the cage."

I watched as he leaned against the wall, red-faced with effort, to kick off his shoes. He raised one foot and laughingly displayed a hole as big as an egg in the heel of his sock.

"I ought to wash your shirt," I said. "It's filthy."

He looked into the little mirror hanging from a nail on the wall and made a face at himself.

"Do you see all that white hair?" he said. "I hadn't noticed it before."

He scratched his neck in perplexity. Then with his shoes in his hand he walked away, looking very awkward in his baggy trousers.

He fixed me something to eat, but as usual he hadn't washed the dishes and brought me a pear on a plate which had been used for sausage.

Later in the afternoon Carlo came around and brought me the latest news from school. Signorina Aiuti had asked him about me and he had told her I wasn't well.

"She asked me what was the matter, and I couldn't think what to reply. Gabriella gave me a strange look. That girl knows everything."

"What else did Signorina Aiuti say?"

"Nothing. She yawned, that's all. Her mother was the one to ask where you lived and whether it was anything serious. But she was quickly distracted, and began talking about her daughters. I was sleepy, and at a certain point I thought I couldn't keep my eyes open."

"You know, we may have to move out of this house."

"Why so?"

"Because we haven't paid the rent for four months and we haven't any money."

"But your father . . ."

"My father makes forty thousand liras a month, and the

rent is twenty. My mother's life insurance money is gone already."

Carlo didn't know what to say. He squeezed my hand and looked at me sympathetically.

"So what are you going to do?"

"I'm not sure. Probably I'll look for a job. In fact, I ought to start looking right away. As for my father, I really don't know."

Carlo got up and began to pace up and down the room.

"There's something I'd like to tell you . . ." he began, but he couldn't seem to make up his mind to go any further.

"What's that?" I asked, looking up at him.

He stood still for a few seconds, staring at the floor.

"Well?"

Wheeling brusquely around he said:

"I went to Gabriella's last night."

Then he came to sit on the edge of the bed and held one of my feet in his hand.

"I went to bed with her," he said, all in one breath. "Do you mind?"

"No."

"I didn't really want to. I realized that when it was all over."

"I don't really care what you do."

"I was hoping you would, at least a little."

"Is that why you did it?"

"Not exactly. I got a kick out of it. But I wanted you, really. I was thinking of you all the time."

He held my foot very tight and leaned over to kiss it.

Just then the telephone rang and I got out of bed and stumbled, with the sheet around me, to answer. Carlo looked regretfully after me. But it wasn't Cesare after all. I slipped back under the covers. Carlo was hanging on to the head of the bed and looking very pale.

"You'd better run along," I said. "I want to sleep."

He got up and went away without a word, his head hanging. I shut my eyes and tried to doze. My father was out and the house was silent. I could hear rain beating against the windows and the full blast of the neighbor's television. My pain was all gone, but I felt weak and infinitely frail. I thought of Cesare in his smoke-filled room, with his legs sprawling under the desk, the ash tray filled with cigarette butts before him and the photographs of Holland behind his blond head. Suddenly I felt I must talk to him. I got out of bed and dialed his number.

"What's the matter?"

From the sleepy but satisfied tone of his voice I knew there was a woman beside him.

"Nothing. I just wanted to say hello."

"You know that when I'm studying I hate to be interrupted."

"I'm sorry," I said, and went back to bed.

But I was too restless to stay there long. I got dressed and went into the kitchen, where I found dirty dishes on the table, unwashed pots and pans in the sink and bread crumbs all over the floor. I rolled up my sleeves an set angrily to work, washing every single piece with hot water and soap and wiping it with a clean dish towel. Then I filled the bathtub and proceeded to throw in my father's dirty shorts, the table napkins and some of my underwear. I scrubbed and wrung until my hands were swollen and painful, my eyes burning and my back aching and streaming with perspiration.

I went out of the house for a breath of air. I stopped to have a cup of coffee and put a coin in the juke box. As I drank I tapped my feet on the floor to the rhythm of a popular song. When I left the café I walked toward Cesare's house. The wet asphalt shone with the reflection of the headlights of passing cars. I turned the corner and stood across from and slightly to the left of Cesare's door. I waited for ten minutes, then changed my position to the right side. After another ten minutes had gone by it seemed as if there were nothing left to do but stand directly across the way.

This time I didn't have to wait for long. After a short time Cesare came out of the house with a short, dark-haired girl wearing a raincoat with the collar turned up all around. Cesare got into the car and opened the door on her side. As she sat down she raised her skirt and I caught a glimpse of the white lace trim of a petticoat. Then she slammed the door and Cesare started the car, totally unaware of my presence.

21

I started going back to school, for the morning classes. In the afternoon I looked for work, which was much more difficult to find than I had imagined. I answered newspaper advertisements and stood in line with a crowd of other girls for secretarial jobs, but invariably I was eliminated because I didn't have a diploma. Sometimes my interview lasted for as long as half an hour, only to end with the news that for the present no one was actually needed. One day I made up my mind to go back to Contessa Bardengo. Perhaps she would be able to help me. When I came into the house she took off her glasses and held out a welcoming hand. At once I told her of my predicament.

"That's too bad," she said. "What about Cesare?"

"I hardly see him any more."

"So you made out all right with the midwife, did you?"

"Yes."

"I'm glad. Now let's see what more I can do. Don't stand there like a stick. Let's have something to drink."

She poured some brandy and sipped it deliberately, staring into the artificial fire.

"I really don't know what to suggest. You know I don't go about very much these days, and I can't appeal to friends whom I've neglected. Have you looked in the newspapers?"

"Yes," I replied. "I went to five or six offices that had advertised for a secretary. But there was a lot of competition and I haven't yet got my diploma."

"Perhaps it's because you look so very delicate. They may have thought you weren't up to hard work."

"You may be right."

"I'm sorry I can't help you. I don't see any possible way."

There were other things on her mind, and she wanted to get rid of me.

"I'll be going," I told her.

She got up and went with me to the door, holding out her hand before she closed it abruptly behind me. I went listlessly down the stairs, staring at one of the stone lions, which seemed to be blissfully asleep with his curly head leaning on his crossed paws.

"Look here! . . ." an impatient voice shouted from above.

I turned around and saw Contessa Bardengo at the head of the stairs, her tight black dress set off by a pearl necklace and with an uncertain smile in her eyes behind the thick lenses.

"How would you like to stay with me?"

Her voice was unsteady but insistent. She beckoned to me, and I went back up the steps, with my feet crunching the wet leaves. She motioned me inside and again shut the door.

"Would you like to be my private secretary? I'd give you board and lodging and a certain amount a month. I sent away the last girl because she was gossipy and a sponge. I hardly know you, but you seem to be a good, quiet sort. I shan't work you too hard. All you'll have to do is to go once or twice a day to the city, to mail letters, do errands and take care of some of the tedious dealings I have with my lawyer. What do you say?"

I didn't know what to reply. I looked at the stains left by humidity upon the walls and at the red carpeting on the stairs which I should be going up and down so many times every day.

[136]

"Your father could go into a home. Didn't you tell me he was quite old and didn't earn enough money for his own support? That way you wouldn't have to worry about him. At first he's sure to kick, but then he'll get used to it. That's always the way."

She poured herself another glass of brandy and went on.

"Let's give it a try," she said, running her hand over my cheek. "If it doesn't work out we'll call it quits, that's all. There's no need of a contract between us. We trust each other, don't we? Think it over and give me a ring when you've made up your mind. There's no hurry."

With these words she went to answer the telephone. I opened the door and once more started away, turning her offer over in my mind.

When I got home I found my father standing in front of his cage with a gleam in his eyes. He took two steps forward and two steps back, walked admiringly around it, half closed his eyes and stretched out his hand to stroke the painted tin cupola.

"It's finished," he said, raising his arms in triumph.

"And very beautiful it is, too," I assented.

"Just look at how well these two colors match one another! Do you see how this motif is repeated below? Isn't that a good idea? It came to me one evening when I was eating supper. I had my back turned to the cage, but it was just as if it were before me. I felt it inside, becoming more alive and beautiful than ever. What did I tell you? I've finished it ahead of schedule, and now I have only to sell it."

"Even if you do sell it we won't be able to pay four months' rent."

"Oh yes we will. You don't understand. I gave it all I had, and that kind of effort has to be paid. It isn't a commercial product; it's a work of art, but art, too, commands pay."

The general effect of the cage was that of a castle. It had crenellated walls, towers, niches, conical roofs and swings with elaborate cords and painted wooden seats in motion inside.

"Join my celebration with a drop of wine," said my father, pouring some into a glass. Then he filled his own and emptied it with a single gulp, clicking his tongue.

"Do you know what we'll do this evening?" he said excitedly. "We'll go out to dinner, the two of us. What do you say to that?"

He hugged me affectionately and then, holding one hand, pulled me toward the door. When we were already outside he stopped short and ran back to the apartment, shouting: "I'm going to put on a clean shirt!" A few seconds later I heard water running in the bathroom. I followed him back into the house and put on my only good dress. It was short and tight, but that didn't matter. I got out some shoe polish and brushed my shoes. My father washed his face and neck before putting on the shirt which I had ironed for him just that morning. Then he stood in front of the mirror to knot his tie.

"Have you enough money?" I called out.

"A certain amount; not too much. We'll go somewhere not too expensive, I know just the place."

"Let's go," I said.

We locked the door and went down the stairs, arm in arm. My father seemed to have recovered his youth. He strode along, talking about his cage and turning to look at his own reflection in the lighted shop windows. We went into a long, narrow, smoky *trattoria*. A family gathered around one of the tables stared at us as we came in, and my father fingered his tie as if to make sure it was in place. A waiter came toward us, carrying a bowl of beans in his hands.

"What a good smell!" my father exclaimed, looking inquisitively around him.

"Two?" asked the waiter impatiently.

"Yes, two. We'll sit over there." And my father pointed to an empty table.

We hung our coats on a hook near the door and sat down. There was a strong odor of fried fish and onions. In a glass case standing against the back wall there were big cuts of red meat and bunches of fresh celery and fennel.

"I'm hungry," my father said.

The waiter came to take our orders and grew impatient when he saw that we were unable to make up our minds.

"I'll have spaghetti."

"Noodles . . . very good."

"No, I've changed my mind. Give me sausage and beans."

"Very good. And the young lady?"

"Well . . . What do you suggest, Father?"

"Take the sausage and beans."

"But I don't like sausage."

"Then take spaghetti."

The waiter grumbled with annoyance as he went away, and we burst out laughing.

"So do you know what?" said my father. "Let's both of us have spaghetti. That's just what I feel like."

We ate the spaghetti, and then both of us ordered boiled meat.

"No fruit," said my father, peering into his wallet. "I haven't got the money. But I *would* like a cup of coffee. How about you?"

"Yes."

"Two cups of coffee, waiter. And our bill."

Beside us two young men were eating in silence, at intervals touching one another's hands. Behind them a stout old woman was talking to a thin, nervous young fellow who didn't seem to be listening. Every now and then she held out a forkful of beans, and he shook his head disgustedly, looking around him with frightened eyes.

The first family we had seen was still sitting near the door.

[139]

Every time anyone came in and left the door open the father boxed his youngest son's ears in order to make him go close it. The father and mother were having a quarrel over their children's heads, while the children tore a bird apart, soiling their faces and fingers. A fair-haired man came in, causing me to start. But it wasn't Cesare. He looked wearily around him, then took off his raincoat and sat down near the unusually silent couple.

"The fellow who just came in looks like Cesare," my father remarked.

"Very true."

"He hasn't called you up lately. And to think that your mother made such a big fuss about your marrying him. 'Let the girl alone,' I always said, but she paid no attention."

I was still looking at the blond-haired man, who was sitting with his back to me. When I half closed my eyes I mistook him for Cesare, and it was wonderful to have Cesare in the same room.

"I've found a job," I said.

"What kind?"

"As private secretary to a lady who lives on the Via Cassia. She wants me to live in the house, and she'll pay me a salary besides."

"And what's to become of me?" he asked, looking down at his spotted hands and at the plastic tablecloth, with its red flower design, which was ripped in several places.

"Oh well," he added, "I'll be quite all right on my own. I'll rent a room, your room. It's a good thing for you to live more comfortably and I'm glad to have you make money. Perhaps you'll find yourself a husband. When I sell the cage I'll buy myself some new suits and pay the back rent. And I still have my work at the office."

He smiled and took two new thousand lira notes out of his wallet with which to pay the bill.

[140]

"The wine was good enough," he said. "By the way, what is the lady's name?"

"Elena Bardengo."

"Sounds impressive. Is she well off?"

"Yes."

"Does she live alone?"

"Yes."

"What do you know about that! So much the better; you won't be overworked. What does she propose to pay you?"

"I don't know. She didn't say. . . . But what if you *don't* sell your cage? What will you do then?"

He clasped his head with his hands in a gesture of dismay. Then, taking hold of himself he said:

"I'm not worried. I've talked to someone about it already, an antique dealer. He says that with a coat of varnish it would pass for something out of the eighteenth century. At that time they had a passion for useless and complicated geegaws. I'm sure to make a sale."

"But if you don't, I say . . ."

"You're talking like your mother. She always saw the gloomy side. I told you the antique dealer was crazy about it, didn't I?"

I shrugged my shoulders.

The fair-haired man was leaning over to eat his dinner. I was tempted to touch his neck, which was slightly red where it was rubbed by his shirt collar. We got up, put on our coats and went out onto the street. It was raining, but so quietly and lightly that I felt as if steam were brushing my skin.

22

Monday. Carrying a big plastic suitcase that had belonged to my mother, I set off for Contessa Bardengo's. My father insisted on escorting me, and he was bowled over by the stone steps, the large rooms, the brocaded tapestries on the walls, the Oriental rugs and the cabinets filled with pieces of silver and china. He nodded as if to say that I had struck it rich. The butler told us to sit down in front of the artificial fire. Then he went away, not without a disgusted look at my father's shabby coat and my plastic suitcase.

"Quite a place," said my father, gazing around him.

"Yes, quite a place."

"And you say she's all alone?"

"So it seems."

"What a shame!"

He scratched his neck in perplexity, stifled a yawn and timidly shifted his feet, without daring to cross them.

"Do you think she might buy one of my cages?"

"Frankly I don't think so."

"Why not?"

"Because she has other things on her mind. She told me herself that she's totally indifferent to what's around her. She lives in the darkness in order not to see things she doesn't like."

"Why doesn't she like them?"

"How should I know? Because they're ugly, I suppose, or because they recall times gone by."

"When she was young, you mean?"

"That's it, the times when she was young."

"I see."

He stood up when he heard the contessa approaching. She was wearing her tight-fitting black dress; her glasses were halfway down her nose and her cheeks were covered with powder.

"How do you do," she said with a smile, holding out her hand to my father.

My father spoke almost at once of his cages, and she listened with a look of amusement on her face. But she made no reply and got up to pour some brandy. My father stared at her white hands, loaded with rings.

"Will you have some?" she asked, offering him a large, balloon-shaped glass.

He nodded and reached for the glass, closing his eyes as he raised it to his lips. His eyes followed her hands as she closed the doors of the false bookcase which served as a bar.

"So you don't mind if your daughter stays here with me?" she said, after taking a sip of brandy.

"Not at all. I'm delighted," said my father, half choking because he had drunk his brandy too fast. He coughed awkwardly and looked with embarrassment into his glass when he saw that she was smiling.

"Then you're giving her into my charge. . . ."

"Yes," he said, solemnly nodding his head.

"She isn't of age, I know," said the contessa. "But you needn't worry about her."

"Of course not," he said obsequiously.

With a sudden access of boldness he laid his hand on hers and spoke again of his cages. But she told him that she wasn't buying anything new for her house.

"And then cages make me sad," she said, raising her voice. "I'm fond of birds, but I like to see them flying about my garden rather than in captivity. I feel quite shut up enough myself without imprisoning a bird."

She threw back her head and emptied her glass of brandy. My father withdrew his hand and with a sudden look of sadness said that it was late and he must go. Contessa Bardengo called the butler and told him to escort my father to the door. Silently my father followed him, but at the threshold he turned around to bid me good-bye, taking my head between his hands and kissing me on both cheeks.

"I'll be calling you up," he said, drawing himself up very erect and then making a stiff bow to the contessa before he stumbled away.

Contessa Bardengo leaned her head against the back of the sofa.

"I'm sorry for him," she said, getting up to pour herself another glass of brandy. "Will you have some?" she added.

"No, thank you."

"It's just as well you shouldn't get into bad habits. I drink all through the day, because it calms my nerves. Don't believe the servants when they tell you that I get drunk. That isn't true. Every time I'm angry at them they blame it on drink. But they're quite wrong. Unfortunately I'm quite clearheaded."

She ran her hand over her dark, fine hair, took off her glasses, breathed on the lenses and wiped them off on her petticoat. Without them her face had a weak, fearful expression. The gold bridge of the glasses had left a red mark on her nose and her eyes seemed to float, naked, in their wide sockets. She batted her wrinkled eyelids and opened her shortsighted eyes.

"Are you happy to be here?" she asked.

"Yes, I am."

"Good. Now let me show you your room. Then, if you feel like it, you can run several errands for me in the city."

She preceded me toward the marble stairs and went up them, swaying on her high heels and holding on to the braided red silk cord with its gilt pendants. At the top of the stairs we went down a hall lined with paintings and mirrors. On either side there were doors, with bronze knobs, one just like the other. We stopped, at last, in front of an open door. Under the window at the far end of the room, between the bed and a desk, I caught sight of my suitcase. Heavy purple curtains partly concealed the window and diffused an unreal, dusty light.

"Here you are," said the contessa, closing the door behind her.

I sat down on the bed, with my head throbbing. The sudden and unexpected silence was overpowering. Outside the four walls of my room I was aware of a silence even deeper, that of the richly furnished great house and the densely planted garden around it. I lay down and shut my eyes. All the objects in the room were strange and incomprehensible. I felt as if someone else were lying on the bed and I were perched in a corner of the ceiling, looking down with amazement at my own supine body. I was roused by the affected voice of Francesco, the butler, telling me that lunch was on the table. I slipped on my shoes, combed my hair and went down the stairs, marveling at how the thick red carpeting muffled my footsteps. The dining room was crammed with furniture and shot through with a pale, tremulous light.

"You may as well keep on going to school in the morning," Contessa Bardengo said, lifting her soup cup to her lips.

Behind her, on the wall, there were some Canton china plates.

"What are you looking at?" she asked, making a face. "The plates? My husband gave them to me one Christmas. Do you like them? They're very valuable. I sit here just so I won't have them before my eyes. Have you ever noticed how obsessive such things can be? They bring back the same memories, over and over."

She wheeled her head around and nodded.

"This house is entirely too full. As soon as I take my eyes off one thing they fall upon another. There's no escape from material possessions. I hate the place. The only part of it I like is my bedroom, because it reminds me of Remo. He's gone away, did I tell you? Don't be surprised if I seem to be upset during the next few days. When he's away I'm always uneasy. I'm afraid he'll never come back."

The telephone rang faintly in the next room, and she started. She dropped her soup spoon and listened, while Francesco's plaintive voice sounded on the other side of the heavy door. A few seconds later, with a face devoid of expression, he returned to the dining room. I fancied I caught a glimmer of malicious joy in his dark eyes as he said that Signora Berci was calling.

"Tell her to go to the devil!" said Contessa Bardengo, twisting her napkin in her hands.

"They spy on me," she explained, taking a drink of wine. "They want to know who's making me suffer, and for whose sake I stay bottled up in the house. The little fools, with their strained, inquisitive faces! They want to see my sagging chin and swollen eyes and laugh about them."

She thrust her fork into the piece of rare meat on her plate, and with nervous haste ate meat and potatoes and salad, all jumbled together. With the feel of the heavy silver knives and forks and spoons in my hand I began to understand what it meant to have money.

"Do you want some fruit?" she asked me roughly.

"Yes, I'd love it."

"I never eat any. Excuse me, but I have to move around. I'm going to pour myself a drop of brandy. Francesco, fetch me the cigarettes from my room."

[146]

Francesco obeyed in leisurely fashion, running his fingers over the sideboard, to make sure it wasn't dusty. A few minutes later I joined the contessa in the drawing room. She sat in front of the fireplace, with a glass in one hand and a shoe in the other.

"My foot hurts," she said, rubbing it with the tips of her fingers. ". . . Francesco is exasperatingly slow. He has a way of pretending he doesn't understand what's wanted so as not to have to make any effort. One of these days I'll get around to firing him. The trouble is that he's been here for fifteen years, ever since my father bought the house. I'd have to give him a big bonus for his long service, and that's a bore."

She took a book down from the shelf near the sofa and leafed through it attentively. I thought she was going to read, but she was only looking for a letter.

"Remo wrote this to me a few months ago," she announced when she had found it, holding it up to her nose. "It still has something of his smell. He has a miserable handwriting, the handwriting of an illiterate. But I wish I could have a letter from him every day. That would cure me. I might even recover my youth. Look at the childish way he writes! He tells me about himself and the way he's living. That's what he used to do a while back. Now he doesn't write any more."

She read the letter through, folded it and, with a sigh, put it back in the book.

"I like you because you know how to hold your tongue," she said, turning abruptly toward me. She stared at me as penetratingly as if she wanted to get inside my thoughts. Then she threw back her head, causing her earrings to tinkle.

"This afternoon I'd like you to go to my lawyer's office. I'll write down the address. Tell him that you're my new secretary and he'll give you some papers for me to sign. Can you drive a car?"

"No."

"Well, you'll learn. Then you can post a letter for me at

the station. I want it to get off as quickly as possible. You must ask when it will be delivered in Naples if it leaves Rome this evening. Why he went to Naples I don't know. He's always hoping to get a part. They make him all sorts of empty promises and he falls for them. Then, when he wakes up to the fact that he's been taken in, he's miserable. It's too bad, that's all. I'm always telling him he's no good for the movies. He doesn't know how to act, even if he is good-looking. And I'll give him all the money he needs, anyhow. What more can he want?"

Nervously she finished her brandy. Her voice was hoarse but pleasant when it was quiet, but disagreeable when she raised it. She gave me the address of the lawyer and the letter to be posted and started to go up to her room.

"I'll see you this evening," she said, but then she turned around and quite unexpectedly slipped two ten thousand lira notes into my hand.

"An advance on your salary," she said. "Buy yourself some clothes. Otherwise I'll soon be tired of seeing you always wear the same thing."

I thanked her and went to get my handbag and make ready to go.

23

When I stopped to read the lawyer's name and found that it was Giulio Guido I couldn't help laughing. As I went up the steps in front of his luxurious house in the Parioli section and rang the bell I tried to remember what he looked like. A tall girl with a pyramid of hair on top of her head opened the door and amiably asked me to come in.

"Do you want to take off your coat?" she asked, eyeing its frayed neck and cuffs.

"No, I'll keep it on."

"As you like," she said with a smile.

She took me into the study, where I stood for several minutes scrutinizing Giulio before he raised his eyes from the papers before him.

"What are *you* doing here?" he exclaimed, with instant recognition. "This is really too funny." And he burst into laughter.

"So you're with that crazy Bardengo woman, are you?"

"Yes, I am."

"Well I'm glad to see you, anyhow. I trust we can get together."

He opened a drawer, pulled out a pale blue folder and began going through some typewritten pages.

"You can take her these," he said. "And tell her that if she doesn't make up her mind to come here in person we'll never get anywhere with this piece of business she cares so much about. Is that clear? . . . Well, well . . . Where did she ever pick *you* up? Not on the street, I trust, the way I did!" He shook his head in amusement. "Well, what's it matter? Your cheeks are pale, though. Does she give you enough to eat? She's so crazy that there's no telling. Just imagine . . ." And he leaned against the back of his chair. "I never thought you'd turn up as a client. You're a smart one, though! She's got plenty of money and when she takes a fancy to someone she doesn't count costs."

He offered me a cigarette, but I said no.

"But even if you're in clover you can always use something extra. There's no such thing as enough money. How about coming to see me sometime?"

"No, I can't do that."

"Why not?"

"I don't want to."

"It would be fun, though. I remember some little white legs . . ." He threw back his head of carefully combed hair and blew some smoke out of his nostrils.

"I must go," I said, getting up, disgustedly. I took the papers from his hand, rolled them up and started out the door.

"What's the hurry?" he asked, rising to his feet.

"I must go."

"Very fussy, aren't you? But that night you seemed to like it, if I'm not mistaken."

I went away very fast, leaving the door open. The girl with the pyramid of hair ran after me.

"Your handbag!" she shouted.

I backtracked, took it from her hand and went on my way. I went into a café and called up Cesare.

"I hear you've got a job," he said, in a tone of satisfaction.

[150]

"Yes, with Contessa Bardengo."

"Well, I've done something for you, after all. If she doesn't give you a square deal, just come to me. I have a certain pull with her, you know."

"When am I going to see you?"

He did not answer right away. Then he grunted:

"I've a lot of studying to do."

"I know."

"Well, if you know, why do you insist?"

"I saw you with that girl in the red raincoat."

"That one?" he laughed. "Why she's my cousin. I swear it. Don't be jealous. You know I like you. I've told you before that we'll stay together until I get married. Then we'll see."

"Do you really want me?"

"Of course. Didn't I just say so?"

"Then when shall we meet?"

"Saturday. How's that?"

"Good."

I left the telephone booth with my face afire. The bus to the station was jammed, and I had to stand in the perspiring crowd. My feet were aching. Suddenly I wanted to have a car and know how to drive it. Outside the bus windows the city seemed to fly by. Shops, houses, men and machines; everything was in rapid motion.

At the station I posted the letter. I lingered in the brightly lighted waiting room, where prospective travelers sat on stone benches, among disorderly piles of parcels and suitcases. I stopped to look at the picture magazines. Inside the newsstand a thin, nervous woman held out change in one hand while with the other she pushed a lock of hair back from her forehead. She looked utterly worn out. As she handed over the papers and magazines her lips moved in arithmetical calculations.

I sat down on a bench beside a man who was guarding a parcel between his legs, as jealously as if he were a setting

[151]

hen. Beside him an old codger was tracing a design on the floor with the point of his umbrella. A baby was crying in his mother's arms. The old man stared at me, without curiosity, and went back to his design, his mouth half open. I listened to the announcements from the loudspeakers, the noise of the baggage trucks and the puffing of the steam engines that were pulling into the station. Every now and then I looked up at the dials of the many neon-lighted clocks and watched the movement of the second hands. When it got to be about eight o'clock I stood up and started back to the house of Contessa Bardengo.

24

As I walked into the classroom I felt Carlo's eyes upon me. I shot him a glance and saw that his lips were moving. I couldn't catch what he was trying to say, so I put down my books and settled into my chair. Behind me Carlo continued to give signs that he was anxious for the lesson to end.

Signorina Aiuti was giving a blackboard demonstration, leaving feathery chalk marks behind her. After a final sweeping gesture she sat down heavily at her desk, took a nail file out of her bag and began to file her nails. Gabriella shook her head, drawing the attention of the whole room upon the shimmering, coppery light of her red hair. Her face was expressionless, but when she turned around to look at Carlo, it was with a self-assured, possessive air.

"Where have you been?" Carlo asked as soon as we were outside the classroom. "I've done nothing but call you up."

"I've moved. I told you I was looking for a job, didn't I? Well, I've found one."

"What kind of a job?"

"As secretary to a rich old lady who lives on the Via Cassia."

"Why didn't you tell me? Yesterday I thought I'd go mad, calling and calling without ever getting an answer."

"Father wasn't home either, that's true. He went with me

when I made the move. The villa is full of all sorts of valuable things, but it's dark as a cave, and she's always drinking."

"Can I call you or come to see you?"

"I don't know why not."

He gave a sigh of relief.

"Let's stop for a hot drink," he suggested.

We ordered two hot chocolates and drank them standing at the counter and looking at our reflections in the mirror above it.

"I'll take you home," he said.

"It's a long way off. I have to take two buses."

"That doesn't bother me. I want to see where you are living."

"Then let's go."

While we were waiting for the bus he told me that his mother had found a job for him, with a rug dealer.

"He's a funny looking fellow with a flat nose, as fat as a hippopotamus. He spouts French and Arabic, both of them very fast, with his lips hardly moving. He'd pay me forty thousand liras a month to start with. What do you say?"

I didn't answer. Just then the bus came along, and for once we found seats. Carlo went on telling me about the offer of a job.

"He calls himself Capuano and comes from Naples, but there's something Oriental about him, above all his nose and his high cheekbones. He might even be a Chinaman. But perhaps his nose was flattened in a boxing match or a fight. Quite a character, I can tell you! He made me stick my face into a pile of rugs. 'Find out for yourself how sweet they smell!' he told me. He said that was the way to tell one rug from another."

We were still talking about the rug dealer when we left the second bus and started to walk toward the villa.

[154]

" 'Villa Letizia,' " said Carlo, reading the name on the gate. "But from the outside it doesn't look very gay."

"It isn't gay inside, either."

"So, can I call you up, Enrica?"

"Certainly."

"When shall I call?"

"Tomorrow."

"What if I feel like calling you later today?"

"This afternoon I'll be going out. I'll be going to the station to post a letter, and then I'm to buy a box of writing paper and some bath towels."

"Does this old dame need a secretary to run errands for her?"

"So far that's all she's given me to do."

"Is she nice, at least?"

"Not always."

"I'd like to know her."

"Good-bye for now. I must go in. Probably she's already started lunch."

"So long then. At what time will you be going to the station?"

"I don't know. It depends on how long it takes me to do the shopping."

"So long."

I waved to him and started up the driveway, crunching the gravel beneath my feet. The cypresses, dampened by the rain, gave out a pungent, resinous smell, and roses were in full bloom along the garden walks. Contessa Bardengo was at the table and motioned to me to sit down.

"Did you post the letter?" she asked anxiously.

"I posted it yesterday evening."

"Of course you did. I'd forgotten. I'll give you another one this afternoon. I haven't had a word from him, and yet he promised he'd write me at least once. Now he's been a whole week in Naples without letting me hear a thing. And he didn't even tell me where he would stay. That's why I have to write to General Delivery."

She ate hurriedly, without paying attention to the food. Francesco waited on us, carrying the heavy silver serving dishes with exaggerated care and deliberation. Whenever he leaned over I could smell the brilliantine on his hair, together with the scent of an effeminate eau de Cologne. Every now and then he wiped his forehead with a perfumed handkerchief.

"I'm going to the dressmaker's this afternoon," said the contessa, leaning her head on her clenched fists. "I like to dress well, for Remo's sake, although he doesn't even notice whether or not I have anything on. I don't know why I do go to the dressmaker's, really. But time drags so when he's away. . . ."

When we got up from the table I handed her the papers which the lawyer had given me the evening before and transmitted his message.

"The idiot!" she exclaimed, taking a cigarette from a newly opened package and offering one to me.

I took it from the package and raised it to my lips. It was long, and soft to the touch. She gave me a light from her lighter, and I inhaled a mouthful of smoke, redolent of honey and tanned leather. At first I was disgusted. Then, as the taste lingered in my mouth, I became accustomed to it and, at the end, as I sipped my coffee I found it actually enjoyable.

"So what did that idiot say? Tell me."

"What idiot?"

"Guido."

I told her again. She laughed, drew her thin lips together and blew the smoke out of her wide nostrils.

"You don't know him," she said. "He'd do anything to break into society. Why do you suppose he offered to be my lawyer for a very small fee? Because he hoped I'd introduce him to some of my friends, to those titled fools I stopped seeing several years ago."

She took off her shoes and put her feet up on the sofa. She was already drinking her second glass of brandy, and behind the thick lenses of her glasses her eyes were gleaming.

"He married Antonietta just because she was a baron's daughter. Now they hate one another."

"Who's Antonietta?"

"She used to be my friend. A good-looking girl who spent her time between the dressmaker's and the hairdresser's, winters at Cortina and summers at Fregene. Skiing and playing cards, those are the only things she knows how to do. Now she's an hysterical old woman, whose only consolation is to spend a fortune on clothes and jewelry. Her husband goes with streetwalkers, everyone knows that. He has a weakness for very young girls. Sometimes he picks them up when they're coming out of school. And he has the nerve to preach to me, the swine!"

She had started out mockingly, but now she frowned as if she wanted to get even with him.

"When he married Antonietta he was pleased with himself for getting into her crowd. Then he found out that there was something still better, a narrower circle to which neither of them had access. Ever since, he's made superhuman efforts to climb this further step. He flatters his clients' wives, stoops to do the lowest kind of favors . . . and, to tell the truth, he seems to have succeeded. These people no longer ignore him. They ask him to their houses, even if it's only in the guise of a lawyer, an adviser. But their welcome is strictly contingent upon his ability to procure annulments and divorces and to make himself agreeable to middle-aged women."

The telephone rang, and her body stiffened with attention. When Francesco failed to call her, she relaxed, poured herself a third glass of brandy and put her legs back up on the sofa.

[157]

"They say he's good at making love. Who knows! I don't care for his kind. He's a vain fool and a hypocrite."

She sighed, leaned her head against the arm of the sofa and shut her eyes. The expression of her babyish, wrinkled face softened, the habitually taut muscles of her neck loosened, her mouth dropped half open and she fell into a sort of torpor. When I saw that she was asleep I crept away and went up to my room.

25

Monday: the day of examinations.

The six ceiling lights were blazing. As a matter of fact, except on unusually sunny days, they were always turned on, because the classroom was in the basement. From the windows we could look up at the legs of the passers-by. At the beginning of the year, curtains had been hung at the windows in order to ward off any such distraction, but they were always pulled aside. We didn't pay much attention to what was happening on the street above, but every now and then one boy passed the word on to another, and they all stared at the legs of a girl or woman with a very short skirt as she went by.

Signorina Aiuti was walking up and down, ill-humoredly, between the rows of desks. She had on a pale blue dress with an artificial flower on one shoulder. Gabriella was sucking her pen, and Signorina Aiuti gave her a withering look. She paused in front of a window to look at a fly that was buzzing against the pane in the search for a way to freedom.

We handed in our papers a few minutes before the bell. Signorina Aiuti raised her unwrinkled white forehead and gave a sigh of relief. She threw her coat over her shoulders and went away, elbowing her way among the students who were chattering in the hall. Carlo went up the stairs beside me. Before we got to the room with the typewriters he squeezed my arm. The loudspeaker started to dictate, and the typewriters to clatter. Gabriella bit her lips because she had made a mistake. With trembling fingers she started rubbing with the eraser and in her haste tore the paper. Anyone could see that she was on the verge of tears.

"Don't stop, keep going!" Carlo shouted from behind her, and she went on typing, with a scowl of concentration on her face.

"*Someone I'll never forget . . .*" said the metallic voice of the loudspeaker above our heads. "*. . . Full stop.*"

"Is there a full stop?"

"Yes, silly."

"*One day I was busy cleaning my spyglasses, when I saw coming toward me . . .*" the voice continued monotonously, while hundreds of fingers ran over the keyboards.

"*May eighth, nineteen hundred and fifty-six. Dear Sir, we have received yours of the sixth . . .*"

I yawned, but went on, piling up several keys on top of each other. When the bell rang we signed our papers and handed them in. Our fingers were aching.

"Stenography next, the most boring subject of all," Carlo whispered in my ear as we moved on to the classroom of Signorina Aiuti's mother, who came to meet us with a feathered hat on one side of her head and a fur-trimmed coat.

"Here are my pets, ready for the test!" she exclaimed. "You aren't scared, are you? I've given you something very easy. Ready with your pencils and your lined paper? Does anyone want to sharpen his or her pencil? I think I have a sharpener with me."

She thrust her hand into her shapeless briefcase and pulled out a worn book, a stubby eraser, a nylon stocking, some rubber bands, a green bottle and, finally, a colored plastic pencil sharpener.

"Here we are!" she said triumphantly, replacing the other

contents of the briefcase, which she had lined up on the desk before her. But no one wanted to sharpen a pencil, and she looked at us with disappointment in her eyes.

"Oh well, never mind," she said, regaining her self-control. "Ready? Well then . . . No, don't write *'Well then.'* Did I ever tell you about the student who . . ."

I noticed how different her voice was from that of her daughter. And yet they made certain identical gestures. Without listening to her story, which I had heard countless times before, I wondered in what ways the other daughter resembled her.

"*To Spanni & Venci, Inc., Rome. Dated, November 21, 1936. Dear Sirs . . .*"

Gabriella was sitting diagonally in front of her paper. I could see that she was quicker than I. When she had finished a sentence she stuck the pencil into her hair and scratched her head distractedly, bending it a little to one side. Signora Aiuti stopped dictating, and I put my head down on the desk while she told a story about how her husband never wanted to get up in the morning. When the examination was over Carlo and Gabriella walked after me out of the room.

"When can we come back for our diplomas?" asked Gabriella.

"Three days from now, that's what she told us."

"Are you coming with me, Carlo?" Gabriella said, clinging to his arm and putting her head on his shoulder.

Carlo looked at me with embarrassment.

"I'm going along," I volunteered.

"Wait a minute," said Carlo, freeing himself from the grasp of Gabriella.

"Aren't you coming?" she said beseechingly.

"Go on," I insisted.

Gabriella looked at him with such pleading eyes that he let her drag him away. I saw them disappear, Gabriella radiant with victory, and Carlo with his head hanging low and his hands stuffed into his pockets. I decided to go see my father before returning to Contessa Bardengo's. I went to the Via Moroni and rang the bell, but nobody came to answer. I rang again, with no result. Just as I was going away I saw a man coming toward me with a key in his hand.

"Are you looking for someone?" he asked.

"I came to see my father. The name is Battini."

"Battini doesn't live here any more."

"Where did he go?"

"I couldn't say. I took the apartment a few days ago."

"Didn't he leave any word?"

"Not with me, but perhaps with the friend who shares the apartment with me. Will you come in?"

"No, thanks. Are you sure you don't know where he is?"

He shrugged his shoulders and threw out his arms, as if to declare his innocence. I said good-bye and went back down the stairs, trying to guess where my father might have gone.

"Perhaps the woman on the floor above can tell you," the new tenant shouted after me. I looked back and saw him insert the key in the lock with casual self-assurance.

"Who?"

"The woman above. Don't you know her? She's always talking about your mother, as if she were her dearest friend."

I shook my head and hurried down the stairs. I paced up and down the street and finally decided to try the wine seller on Piazza Bologna.

"Hello there, young lady," he called out from behind a row of bottles.

"Have you seen my father?" I asked him.

"Not for some time. I was beginning to wonder whether he was on the wagon."

His eyes ran curiously from my feet to the top of my head.

"Prettier than ever," he observed. "Do you want some wine?"

"No. I must be getting along. If you see my father, tell him to call me up. He knows where to reach me."

"Very well. Good luck!" he shouted after me as I ran to catch the bus.

I reached the villa just in time for lunch.

"Your father called you," said Francesco as I sat down.

"Did he leave a message?"

"He gave me an address, and said you could find him there."

I ate distractedly, listening to Contessa Bardengo's running conversation. She talked to pass the time away, occasionally pausing, forgetful of my presence and of that of the food, to stare into empty space. Francesco came up and touched her arm with the edge of the tray, causing her to jump.

"Yes, the meat pie was delicious. Please tell Germana. But I won't have any more."

The night before, I had met Francesco in the hall, coming out of the room of the young chambermaid, Pina. He had bowed politely, stifling a yawn. Now he looked at me with fear in his eyes, as if he thought I might be going to say something about it to Contessa Bardengo.

As we sat over our coffee in the drawing room the front doorbell rang and the countess paled. A youthful voice rang out in the anteroom.

"It's Remo!" she exclaimed. "I'll be right back."

I sat stiffly, not knowing what to do. A few moments later Remo stood in front of me, holding out his hand with an interrogative air.

"Hello there," he said, looking around for the contessa.

"She'll be here in a minute," I said.

He sat down in the place she had just vacated.

"What's your name?" he asked.

"Enrica."

"How's her mood?" he whispered.

"She's nervous."

He made a face and proceeded to look me over.

"It's so dark in here," he said suddenly, getting up and starting to pull back the curtains.

"She wants it that way," I told him.

"I know. She's afraid I'll count her wrinkles. I don't give a' hang about them. I don't even notice. Do you think of yourself as being young? I don't. But she's always telling me so. As far as I'm concerned, everyone's as old as he feels. Don't you agree?"

I nodded, and he came back to sit on the sofa. Out of the pocket of his leather jacket he produced a tiny transistor radio.

"How do you like that?" he asked me.

"It's a beauty."

"She gave it to me for my birthday two years ago. You ought to hear the tone."

A shrill voice emerged, accompanied by a band.

"What do you say?"

"Wonderful!"

"Where the devil did she go?" he said just as the contessa came into the room.

Her cheeks were covered with powder and her lips bright red. She had puffed her hair high up on her head and put on a pair of glasses I had never seen before, with white rims decorated with sequins. They proceeded to embrace. Remo clung to her shoulders, digging his fingers into her flesh, while she helplessly abandoned herself. I got up and left the room. Looking back, I saw them in one another's arms, exchanging a passionate kiss.

26

I went back to the secretarial school to get my diploma. The directress received me in the outer office and took the precious paper out of a tall pile.

"You'll surely find a job," she told me. "The name of our school is the best recommendation."

She gave me a motherly smile and immediately turned around to look for something in the bookcase behind her. I went away with the diploma under my arm in the direction of the Violo del Cinque, where my father had moved. The trees along the Tiber had just been pruned, and branches lay stacked up along the sidewalk, giving out an odor of freshly cut wood and trodden leaves. The river was yellow and swollen with the March rains.

I went through a narrow, dark doorway, which smelled of cabbage and mold. The plaster on the walls was eaten away by the dampness. I walked up the high stone steps all the way to the top floor, where a young woman with a baby in her arms came to answer my knock.

"Does Annibale Battini live here?"

"Who?"

"B-a-t-t-i-n-i."

"You mean the old man with the bird cages?"

"Yes, that's the one."

She smiled and stepped aside.

"He's quite crazy, you know. Here everyone calls him 'that bird.' The trouble is he litters the floor with bits of wire. He's taken to working on the terrace, because my mother told him she was tired of sweeping his room. There was quite a mess to clean up, I can tell you."

The baby began to cry and she pressed him to her breast, stroking his head.

"I should think he'd be cold outside," she said, pointing to a closed door. "But he's good-natured, all right. Never makes a sound."

"Doesn't he go to the office?"

"Oh, yes, works for an insurance company, doesn't he?"

As soon as I pushed open the door I saw him, with a row of nails between his lips, in front of a cage larger and more ambitious than any he had made before. He had on his coat, and a wool scarf wrapped several times around his scrawny neck, but his nose was red with cold. He didn't hear me come in, and continued to work on his cage, with the usual bottle of wine standing in a geranium pot beside him.

"Father!"

He started, raised his head, took the nails out of his mouth and came over to embrace me.

"Aren't you frozen?" I asked him.

"No. Why?"

"Look out, or you'll find yourself down with pneumonia."

"Always prophesying doom, just like your mother!" he said crossly, pushing me away.

"Anyone else would say the same thing."

"Maybe so, but I'm in very good health. This is just the place for me. I have complete privacy, and besides I like having the sky rather than a roof over my head."

"What if it starts raining?"

"Then I stop working," he said, shrugging his shoulders. "Or else I take some small piece inside that needs to be filed."

"Did the landlord throw you out of our old house?"

"I realized I couldn't go it there alone," he said, shooting a sidelong glance at the cage. "Here I pay eight thousand liras a month for the room, and have money left for my meals."

"You still go to the office, then?"

"Why not? There's no reason for them to fire me. They're used to seeing me around. And I like living here. It's a happy little family. If it weren't for the baby crying it would be perfect."

"Did you sell that other cage?"

Instead of answering he changed the subject.

"How are you making out with the contessa?"

"All right. Look at this, will you?" And I held out my rolled-up diploma.

On the scroll of imitation parchment, decorated with laurel wreaths and sheaves of wheat, my father read the news that Enrica Battini had satisfactorily completed the study of typing and stenography.

"Good girl!" he said, picking up the bottle and offering it to me. "There are no glasses," he explained. "But have a drink to celebrate. Go ahead . . . I'll finish it."

I upturned the bottle, but almost as soon as I started to swallow, my father snatched it out of my hand, causing some of the wine to spill on my coat.

"What in the world are you doing?"

"I'm sorry. I was afraid you'd drink it all up. And I have no more money to spend on wine today."

With his handkerchief he wiped off the lapel of my coat. His face had suddenly darkened. Leaning over the wall he looked down at another identical terrace.

"That girl is always washing!" he grumbled.

I leaned over and saw a young heavy-set girl, with her sleeves rolled up over her chubby arms, reaching toward a wire that looked as if it might collapse under the weight of the laundry hung upon it.

"She has a good voice, though," said my father.

The girl hung up one last pair of socks with two clothes-pins. Then, holding the empty laundry basket against one hip, she disappeared through a narrow door.

"It's nice to have a terrace," I remarked.

"So you like it here, too."

"Yes, I do."

"When I'm tired of working on my cage I can lean over and see the world. I know all the cats of the neighborhood, and the people too. Do you see that kitchen with the window opening onto the street? Two women live there, a mother and daughter who quarrel all day long. The daughter's got herself pregnant, and the mother does nothing but scold her. Everyone can hear; some people laugh, and others slam their windows. And there, in that basement, six people are crowded in together. Luckily the father and the oldest son go out to work. The little ones play on the street, and only a hunchbacked old woman is left at home. Every now and then she comes to the door with a pot in her hand and spits onto the pavement."

He laughed, took a small pack of papers out of his pocket, laid one out on the wall, filled it with a pinch of tobacco and rolled himself a cigarette.

"Have a puff?" he said.

"No, thanks."

"This tobacco is quite a mixture. There are iron dust, wood shavings, bits of string and God knows what else in it."

He inhaled a mouthful of smoke, then blew it out, coughing. We had no more to say and he seemed impatient to get back to work. I stayed a few minutes more, deadened by the cold, staring at the dripping, wind-blown clothes swinging from the wire on the terrace below.

"I'll be going," I said at last.

"Good-bye. Come to see me again."

I went back into the house, where the baby was crying as he clung to his mother. She dandled him on her knee and reached over him to peel potatoes on the kitchen table.

"Always hungry," she complained. She laid down the knife, unbuttoned her blouse, pulled out a white breast, heavy with milk. The baby thrust forward his head, with closed eyes, looking with both his mouth and fingers for something to suck. Finally he found the nipple and took possession of it, swallowing greedily, without stopping even to breathe. His mother smiled at me as I moved toward the door.

"Mind you don't stumble on the stairs in the dark," she warned me. "Go straight down and you'll find the front door. You'll have to slide back the bolt. Good night and good-bye."

"Good night," I answered.

I found Carlo sitting on the last step.

"How did you know I was here?" I asked him.

I followed you when you left school with the diploma under your arm. I called after you, but you didn't hear."

"Why didn't you follow me upstairs?"

"I thought I'd rather wait for you here."

His tightly rolled diploma was as slender as a stick, and he was tapping it against his knees.

"I'll see you home," he said.

"Let's go, then."

"You know I talked again to that rug man, Capuano. He really seems to want to take me on. The only trouble is I'll be busy all day long and never have a chance to see you. I don't like that idea at all. Up to now I could count on seeing you at school. But after this it won't be so easy."

"One can get used to anything. I've heard you say that yourself."

"That may be true. But it won't be any fun."

"What do your parents say?"

"They're glad for me to be independent."

"Let's stop for a hot drink."

It was a humble café composed of a single big room with sawdust on the floor and posters advertising beer and Coca-cola decorating the walls. A man was yawning behind the counter. We ordered two cups of coffee. Carlo went to look at the far end of the room, where three rows of chairs were lined up for people who wanted to look at television. He called out to me to join him.

"Let's sit down. You must be tired. Tell the fellow to bring us the coffee back here."

The chairs were lined up in such a way that they might have been in church. Before us, on a metal support, stood the TV with its convex glass front, momentarily unlit and gray.

"This place smells like a latrine."

Carlo squeezed my hands. He opened his mouth as if to say something, but not a sound came out. His lips were trembling.

"Would you marry me?" he said all of a sudden.

Looking over at him, I saw that he had suddenly turned very pale.

"I have the assurance of a job, and if we were to put our two salaries together . . ." he continued uncertainly.

"I don't think it's such a good idea."

"Why not?"

"I don't think so, that's all."

He lowered his head and bit his lip.

"Shall we get going?" I said.

"I need to make love with you, just once more. What do you say?"

"I say no."

"Please. We don't have to see one another again. But just this one last time . . ."

He was breathing heavily, and I bowed my head.

"Will you?" he insisted.

"All right."

He dropped my hand, leaped to his feet and went to pay for the coffee. I met him at the door, and pulled on the new gloves given to me by Contessa Bardengo.

27

"The contessa is in her room and doesn't want to see anyone," Francesco told me.

"Has she had lunch?"

"No. She stayed shut up all morning. She wouldn't even
have the maid come in to make her bed."

"What's wrong?"

"I don't know. Probably it's something to do with that
fool . . . you know who I mean, don't you?"

He stared at me out of his crafty eyes. Then he slowly
pulled on the white gloves which he wore to serve at the
table. I sat down and ate, without any appetite. The whole
afternoon stretched out ahead of me and I didn't have anything to do. Should I wait for the contessa to call me or go
into the city on my own?

After the last sip of coffee I went up to my room. I pulled
open the curtains in order to have more light and stood in
front of the mirror, combing my hair. The villa was immersed
in silence. Outside a high wind was blowing. I looked at the
bending cypresses, the clump of flattened rhododendrons
and the stripped oleanders. Only the magnolia tree seemed
to be standing up under the repeated gusts. I felt cold and
stepped under the hot water of the shower to get warm. Then
I walked up and down the room in my wrapper. I had an

urge to call Cesare, but I knew that Francesco was mounting guard over the telephone. When he had nothing to do he sat down beside it, put on his glasses and read the morning paper. He began with the want-ads on the last page and worked his way back through the death and marriage notices, the accounts of local accidents and crimes, to the editorials and headlines. By the time he reached the front page he let the paper slip down onto his knees and as often as not fell asleep.

I lit a cigarette, but it went out after my first puff and I found I had no matches. I went out into the hall, trying to accustom my eyes to the darkness. I thought I remembered seeing a cigarette lighter in Contessa Bardengo's private sitting room, next-door to the room where she was supposedly resting.

The only light was that filtering in between the half-closed shutters. A thick bunch of flowers, stuffed into a vase, gave out a strong odor of pollen. I started to pick up the lighter, and in doing so knocked my knee against the glass table. The sound rang out like a bell in the silence. Hurriedly I lit my cigarette and started to go away.

"Is that you, Enrica?" said a voice from the bedroom.

"Yes."

"Come here, will you?"

When I opened the door I could see only the shadowy forms of the furniture and a lighter object, which I realized must be the bed. From it a waving arm beckoned to me.

"Sit down," said the contessa.

I sat down on an armchair at the foot of the bed. Little by little I made out the outline of the rumpled bedclothes and that of the contessa herself, in a transparent nightgown. On the bedside table were two brandy bottles, one empty and the other newly opened, a bathroom mug, a box of sleeping pills and her familiar eyeglasses.

[173]

"I have a terrible headache," she said in an unsteady, plaintive voice.

"Perhaps you should have something to eat."

"I'm not hungry."

She stretched out a hand, on which she wore two diamond rings, and grasped my arm.

"Remo's gone away," she breathed into my face. Then she fell back onto the pillow. By now I could distinguish her face, which without make-up looked younger than usual.

"Oh well, he'll be back," I answered weakly, just for the sake of something to say.

"No, he won't. He's found someone else to support him."

"Who's that?"

"A man. An American film director."

Once more she raised herself on her elbow and dug perspiring fingers into my arm.

"I must manage to survive from today until tomorrow," she said. "After that I'll get along. The first day is the worst."

She poured some brandy into the bathroom mug, which was smeared with toothpaste, and then, because her hand was shaking spilled half of it on the bed.

"Let me pour it," I said, taking the bottle out of her hand.

"Stay here," she murmured into my ear. "I need somebody to talk to. . . . I'm burning up inside because I want him so badly."

She fell silent, then put her hand up to her mouth to hold back a sob. Her forehead was contracted with pain.

"I shall leave this house," she said, kicking the covers. "I hate this bed, that door, which I stared at all morning long in the hope that he would come through it. . . . An American film director, imagine! . . . That I should be jealous of an American film director! I don't mind sharing Remo with someone else. The only thing I can't bear is the idea of never seeing him again."

She lit another cigarette. The odor of brandy was nauseating. I looked at her breasts, which were as small as those of a young girl and at the whiteness of her thighs, visible under the tulle nightgown.

"An American film director, Enrica! How do you imagine such a man? Is he very tall? Fair haired? I know that he's just a little older than myself. Do you suppose he has a mouthful of gold teeth and all the little ways of doing things that one expects from a man that buys young boys for his pleasure? I can't understand it. A film director! It isn't for the money, I'm sure. I never refused him anything. Probably the fellow has promised him a part. Remo always falls for that. Probably he's letting that stupid film director kiss his neck in return for some vague promise. . . . Won't you have a drink of brandy? It goes straight to the heart, you know. It makes the heart pound, but you feel better. I'm feeling better already. I'm actually happy, you can't imagine how happy! So happy I could cry."

Just then the telephone rang close by. I had not noticed that there was one in the room, because it was half buried in the bedclothes.

"You answer," said the contessa. "I'm not at home to anyone, not even to Remo."

"Hello," I said into the telephone. "No, I'm sorry, she's out." And with that I hung up.

"I haven't answered all day," she told me. "I pick up the receiver, and when the voice isn't his, I just put it down."

She groped for her cigarettes.

"Will you light one for me?" she asked.

I took one of the long, filter-tipped cigarettes for myself as well, and breathed in its molasses-like aroma. The contessa let hers hang between her lips and threw back her head. Her body was waxen white, with a network of blue veins crisscrossing its smooth surface.

We smoked in silence. The room was overheated, and I was gradually overcome by a feeling of lethargy. I let myself go in the velvet upholstered armchair and stretched my legs out in front of me. The contessa shifted onto one side, turning her back to me, and leaning her head on one hand. I was nearly asleep when she called out imperiously:

"Go away!"

I got up, rubbing my eyes.

"Go away!" she repeated. "I need to be alone."

"I'm going," I answered.

"A film director!" she muttered. "It's crazy for me to lie here and try to imagine what he's like. I must see him and find out. Ridiculous, isn't it? Tell Francesco to bring out the car. As soon as it's dark I'll drive into the city. I know where to find them. . . . Go along . . ."

I opened the door and shut it slowly behind me. In the hall I met Francesco, who glanced at me mockingly. I gave him the contessa's order. Then I went back to my room and threw open my window. The sudden influx of cool air made me shiver. The day was nearly over, and a red edge was forming around the clouds behind the magnolia tree in the garden.

28

The next day Remo came back, all smiles, with the tiny transistor radio tucked into his back coat pocket. He ran up the stairs, to a musical accompaniment, and disappeared into the contessa's bedroom.

"Little idiot! Son of a bitch!" muttered Francesco, following him with a look of hate in his eyes. "He doesn't even bother to say hello. Thinks he's master of the house, does he?"

With that he shut the door and went into the kitchen. I grasped at the chance to call Cesare.

"Hello there!" he said. "Where in the world have you been?" There was honest surprise in his voice.

"When am I going to see you?" I countered.

"I took the exam and passed it," he said triumphantly.

"Good. So you're no longer pressed for time?"

"Oh yes, I am. Now it's wedding preparations."

"When is the wedding?"

"Very soon."

"When?"

"In ten days."

I swallowed hard, feeling a lump in my throat.

"What's the matter there?" he said from the other end of the wire. "You knew it was coming."

"Yes, but I didn't know it would come so soon."

"Nini wanted to advance the date. I don't know why, but she's in a hurry. As if I were going to run away! . . ." He laughed and then added: "Do you mind very much?"

"You know I do."

"You must really care for me. Too bad I had to get myself engaged. We might have been happy as husband and wife. What do you say?"

"When shall I see you?"

"I don't know if there's time."

"But you promised that we'd see each other once before you got married."

"That's true. Let's say . . . how about Tuesday of next week? Is that all right?"

"Very good."

"So long."

"So long."

In the mirror I saw Francesco's crafty face break into an ironical smile.

"She wants me to serve lunch for two. After a whole day when she didn't eat a thing! And at this hour! That idiot boy might have taken the time into account!"

With abrupt, angry gestures he began to set the table. I lit a cigarette, then pulled back the curtains to look into the garden. The hard, shiny leaves of the magnolia tree were opening up around the white buds. The grass was soft and fresh and blue-green. Spring had come. I heard footsteps in the room and saw the two of them approach, walking close together. She had thrown her arm protectively across his shoulder and with her fingers was touching his hair.

"Enrica!" she called out. "Did you see who's here?"

"Yes, I saw him go upstairs a few minutes ago."

"He's left that director. It seems he was a stingy little shrimp. Remo, tell Enrica what you just said to me about him."

Remo shrugged his shoulders, put his hand in his pocket

and turned on the radio. A voice announced Modugno's *Nel blu dipinto di blu.*

"No music just now, my sweet," she said with annoyance. "We want to talk."

Disappointedly he turned it off, and the smile left his face. He had olive skin, a well-cut mouth and evenly shaped eyebrows, whose black curves might have been traced by a piece of coal.

"Tell me the story about the director again," she said. "It's really funny."

Remo looked with embarrassment in my direction. I started to go away, but Contessa Bardengo held me back.

"You must stay," she said. "I want him to tell you how he handled the director. I needn't have worried. . . . Are you glad you're back, you sweet thing?" she went on, turning toward him. "Tell me again that you're glad."

Remo timidly lowered his eyes.

"He's afraid to shock you," said the contessa.

"I'm going. . . ." I insisted.

"No, don't do that. He mustn't be shy with you. You know all about us. And besides, he's just your age. . . . Remo, did you know that Enrica is just as old as you?"

Remo raised his languid eyes, whose expression was that of a suspicious child. Surreptitiously he thrust his hand once again into his pocket and turned on the radio, very low. A nasal voice spoke out of his chest announcing a program of "Music for People at Work."

"For heaven's sake, turn that off!" said the contessa, putting her hands over her ears. "Apparently you do intimidate him, Enrica. You'd better go, after all."

Remo did not raise his head as I walked away. I went into the garden. The wind was cold, but the air was fragrant with resin and new grass. My shoes sank into the mud, as I brushed against the bushes, heavy with buds. I picked some bitter-sweet sweet peas, then walked up a long alley and

[179]

went to sit on a bench in the farthest corner. I shut my eyes and took a deep breath. The wind brought with it not only the smell of the earth but that of the freshly tarred road as well. Every now and then I had a whiff of the gasoline of a passing car. I turned my face up to the sun and closed my eyes. I could imagine the inside of the villa, Contessa Bardengo's body, the spots of brandy on the sheet, the sharp but infantile profile of Remo, Francesco's big, white-gloved hands. It's a crazy, senseless life, I said to myself. I really ought to look for another job, to make myself a life quite different from this one. By the time I opened my eyes I had made up my mind. Treading on the new grass, I walked slowly back to the villa.

29

Monday. I lay on my bed, thinking how in twenty-four hours I should be making love, for the last time, with Cesare. I could see every detail of his room—the photographs of Holland on the wall, the imprint of his body on the sheet—and smell the familiar odor of his skin. He was slipping his blond-haired legs between mine. . . . He was heavy when he lay on top of me, but I never noticed until he rolled over onto his side, with a look of mingled sleepiness and satisfaction. While he buried his face in the pillow and slept, I stared up at the design on the ceiling. The telephone rang, and he stretched out an arm to reach for it over my body. Nini talked to him about the wedding, the expense of sending out invitations and giving a party. He answered in a hypocritically genial manner, with his eyes closed and one finger tickling my neck. With a single gesture he put down the receiver and hoisted himself on top of me again. I felt his hot breath in my ear and the pervasive warmth of his body.

I was aroused by the shrill voice of Contessa Bardengo, calling from her bedroom.

"I'm coming," I answered.

"Enrica!" she shouted impatiently.

I ran a comb through my hair and hurried to see what she might want. She met me at the door, in her slip, with cold cream on her face and a yellow towel wrapped around her hair. Squinting, because she was without her glasses she said:

"What were you doing? Sleeping?"

"No."

"Remo and I are going out to dinner tonight, and Remo wants you to come along. That way people won't gossip about him and me; they'll imagine he's your lover. He's promised to dress up. Last year I gave him a dark blue suit which he's never worn. It's very becoming; you'll see. I remember the day when the tailor's assistant came for a fitting and he tried to stand still in front of the mirror. What a boy!"

"But . . ." I started to protest.

She cut me short by saying that Remo would call for us at eight-thirty.

"We'll go in my car. Put on that black dress in which you look so well." And with that she slammed the door.

While I was dressing I heard the contessa sing. Remo arrived punctually, wearing the dark blue suit, whose jacket was short and tight now that he was a year older. He came up the stairs looking at his shoes. His hair had been cut, and he looked thinner and older than the day before. Before we left he took a last scowling look at his reflection in the mirror, facing first one way and then the other.

"It's a tight fit, don't you think?" he said to Contessa Bardengo.

"No, I don't. I'd call it perfect."

"Let's go," he said, catching hold of my wrist.

We sat all together on the front seat of the custom-built sports car. The contessa was at the wheel, with one hand on Remo's hip, while one of his arms encircled my shoulders. She steered with two black-gloved fingers. Her somewhat hawklike profile was reflected on the windshield, and the sequins on her eyeglasses twinkled in the light thrown by passing cars.

Remo reached out a hand to turn on the car radio. The contessa made a gesture of annoyance, but did not prevent him. Soon the music was deafening. Remo stuck his head out the window and looked at the street, as happy as a child.

The restaurant was in a basement. It consisted of a chain of dimly-lit rooms, one after the other, with vaulted ceilings, tiled floors and wine bottles lining the walls. Remo looked timidly around him. We sat down at a corner table, near the orchestra, which was playing in a subdued tone.

"This is knockout!" Remo exclaimed.

"Do you really like it? What will you have to eat?"

"Something special."

"Lobster?"

"No, something more special than that."

"How about some roast dog?"

Remo laughed until it seemed as if he would burst out of his collar. His eyes were bright and his cheeks flaming.

"Let's drink some champagne. What do you say?"

Remo was crumbling a piece of bread in his hands. Every now and then he stuck a little ball of it into his mouth. The bottle of champagne was soon empty, and we ordered another. Contessa Bardengo had taken off her glasses. She was less concerned about eating her own dinner than she was about Remo's enjoyment of his. As he ate she stared at him blissfully.

"How about some game?" she asked him. "Have you ever eaten boar? Or would you rather try quail?"

"I don't know," said Remo, laughing defensively.

"What about you?" the contessa asked me.

"I'd love some boar."

"I'll have some too," Remo put in.

"Good. Boar for both of you."

"What about yourself?" said Remo.

"I'm not hungry. I'm happy to watch you eat."

The waiter brought the boar. Remo cut into a thick slice

covered with dark sauce and stuffed it voraciously into his mouth. He tried to spear an olive, but it fell onto the table-cloth.

"Messy boy!" said the contessa, as if he were her son.

Remo picked up the olive with his fingers and stuck it between his teeth. He drained his glass of wine and poured himself another. The contessa smiled encouragingly and patted his hand.

The orchestra was playing more loudly. A man with curved shoulders, wearing dark glasses, sat down near our table and played an electric guitar. I looked disgustedly at the fruit cup in front of me. The tinned grapes and cherries were floating in a mass of liquefied whipped cream

"Are you sleepy, Enrica?" asked the contessa.

"No."

"I feel like dancing," said Remo, tapping his heels on the floor.

"Let's dance, then," said the contessa, getting up and grasping his hand.

A small space among the tables was reserved for dancing. I saw the contessa's thin body clinging to Remo's, her green dress pressed against his dark blue suit. Beside them two elderly Americans were improvising an elaborate figure. Another couple, very young, moved deliberately from one tile to another, as if it required immense effort to lift their feet from the floor. With his eyes closed, the guitar player was singing. Every now and then he laid aside his instrument and drank some beer. He was wearing green trousers and a black jacket with gilt buttons.

The vase of flowers at the center of the table trembled in time with the cadenced steps of the dancers. There was some champagne left in the glasses. I took a sip and lit one of the long cigarettes which the contessa had left behind her. Over the noise of the orchestra I could hear the shrill voice of a woman sitting behind me. Between spasmodic laughs she was sporadically carrying on a loud conversation, which seemed as if it would never come to an end. She laughed and laughed, hiccoughing at the same time, while the two men on either side of her looked, with a bored air, around the room.

"You shouldn't be so stiff when you dance," the contessa said to Remo when they came back to the table.

"I don't claim to be a dancer," he protested.

"You are one, though, except that you hold yourself as stiffly as if you expected to fall. You should let yourself go with the music . . . swing and sway. There are things no American film director can teach you."

Remo hung his head somberly. The contessa put her hand under his chin and blew him a kiss.

"Have I hurt your feelings?" she asked.

"No."

"Go dance with Enrica. She mustn't be a mere spectator. That's no fun."

Remo shot me an annoyed glance, but the contessa insisted.

"Go on. Probably she dances better than I do. You'll certainly be a better matched couple."

Remo got up and walked ahead of me toward the dance floor. The orchestra was going full blast, obliterating the sound of the guitar. The guitar player, with the curved shoulders, was barely strumming his instrument, with his eyes cast down, a cigarette hanging between his lips and a lock of shiny hair bobbing up and down on his forehead.

"You're a good dancer," said Remo.

"So are you."

He held me lightly.

"I've had too much to drink," he said. "My head is reeling."

"Mine isn't."

"You make me feel ashamed, do you know?"

"Why?"

"Because of that silent stare."

"The first time I saw you, you weren't ashamed."

"That's true. She's the one that puts me to shame." And he pointed at the table where we had left Contessa Bardengo. She was drumming with her fingers on the table and staring at them as if she were fascinated by the gleam of her rings.

"Haven't you any family?" Remo asked me.

"I have my father, but he's an old man."

"And you aren't engaged?"

"No. The man I love is getting married in ten days."

He held me tight, and I could feel the hardness of his chest underneath the jacket.

"What interests you most in life?" he asked, drawing back in order to look me in the face.

"I don't know. Love, I suppose."

"What I like is music. She doesn't like me to turn on the radio. At home I keep it going the whole time. I even take it to bed."

"To bed?"

"Yes. Making love isn't everything. I like to be loved, all right, but not so wildly. She wears me out. I'd like to be an actor, to be rich and famous."

"Is that why you ran away?"

"Yes. But then I realized that I was better off with her. She's really fond of me. She's always giving me presents and she never scolds."

"What will you do when you come of age?"

"I don't know. I'd like to break into the movies, but it's not easy. I wish I could play some instrument, but I've never learned how."

"Where does your family live?"

"At Centocelle. You know, just outside the city."

"Do you have any brothers and sisters?"

"Yes, six . . . My mother's always yelling at them about

something. I can't bear it. Ever since I can remember she's been nursing babies and mopping up the floor."

"And what does your father do?"

"It's hard to say. He always shifting from one thing to another."

The music stopped and Contessa Bardengo beckoned to me.

"You left me alone for an awfully long time," she protested with a smile. "What were you talking about?"

"About our families."

"Poor Remo! How many brothers and sisters have you got? Eight or ten, isn't it? And to think that I was an only child, rattling about in a big house! . . ."

She took Remo's hand and squeezed it. But Remo was all ears for the next piece of dance music and paid no attention. When the music began he made a face.

"Always the same old thing! Let's go somewhere else."

"Where do you want to go?"

"To a place where we can dance."

"But there's dancing here."

"There's too much of a crowd."

"All right, then; let's go."

We piled back into the car and drove to the entrance of a night club on the Via Veneto. A neon sign blinked on and off at the head of a stairway winding down between a church and an office building.

"There's a strip tease act here," said the contessa.

"Is that fun?"

"Not too much. After you've seen it once it isn't very exciting."

Remo shrugged his shoulders and adjusted his tie. We went down into the fake catacomb, with its low ceiling and frescoed walls, and the ancient Roman jars and vases, covered with barnacles and calcareous deposits, standing against them.

"It's stuff they dredged up from the bottom of the sea," said the contessa, running a finger over the neck of a long, narrow vase with a pointed bottom, which was resting on a metal tripod.

The darkness was such that we could make out very little around us. I found myself beside a group of men who were smoking and drinking and looking at the dancers. Remo and the contessa were on the dance floor, in a tight embrace, with a ray of yellowish light falling from the ceiling upon them. I stifled a yawn. My eyes strained to penetrate the darkness, but I could see nothing but black masses and areas on every side. There was no way of making out the shape of the room. The languid notes of a hit song seemed to drift down from a platform, and the only sound was that of lightly moving feet.

I leaned back against the upholstery of my seat and closed my eyes. My fingers were closed about a corner of the embroidered tablecloth, which took me back in my memory to a time long gone by. I was about nine years old, and my mother was teaching me to sew. She wanted me to wear a thimble and I wouldn't do it. She put a needle between my fingers, unwound some thread from a spool and handed it to me. I tried to thread the needle, but my hand was shaking and the needle fell to the floor, causing my mother to burst out laughing. I was angry, and tried over and over again until the thread was black and raveled. My mother took the whole thing out of my hands and with a deft gesture slipped the thread through the eye of the needle. Then she showed me how to take big horizontal stitches. All the while she talked to me about the farm where she had lived when she was small. She told me about her cousins and how they split open lizards and stuffed them with leaves. They were always cutting up animals, she said, in order to discover how they were made. She used to follow them around, for the excitement, but at the last minute she would turn her head away while they laughed and called her a lily-livered girl. Once, in order to prove herself, she had wrung the neck of a chicken with her own hands. But the chicken was not dead and fluttered away, with terrifying squawks, across the barnyard. Her father saw her from the house and slammed shut the window out of which he was looking. A short time later he came out with his sleeves rolled up and an angry expression on his face, and she ran to hide in the barn, where he failed to find her. But that evening, as they sat around the kitchen table, he lifted her up bodily from her seat and gave her a cuff that sent her reeling against the wall. He sent her to bed without any supper, and she had to bite her lips all the way up the stairs in order not to cry. Later her younger brother brought up an onion and slipped it into her bed. She hid her head under the covers and nibbled it hungrily. Nothing in her later life, she assured me, ever tasted as good as that onion. In telling me this story she made a wrong stitch and had to bite off the thread and begin all over. This time I was the one to laugh. I took another piece of thread and threaded the needle without difficulty. Ever after that I felt as if I had always known how to sew.

The music stopped abruptly and a spotlight was focused on the center of the dance floor. The dancers scattered into the surrounding darkness, and their place was taken by a heavily made-up girl with long artificial eyelashes and silvery hair held up by a fake-diamond pin. As the music grew gradually louder, she reached for the zipper of her skirt and let it fall to the floor. The spotlight played upon her while she toyed with the top part of her dress and dropped it off in the same way. Lifting her legs in time with the music she peeled off her stockings. From then on the process was like peeling an onion. After the petticoat came the brassière, then the underpants, the garter-belt and finally the G-string. When she was completely naked the band stopped playing, except for a single drum, which went on like that of a circus. With a final coquettish gesture the girl raised her hand to her neck and let her silvery, almost white hair cascade down over her shoulders.

Remo puffed at a cigarette and with intent eyes followed her every motion. The contessa did not so much as look at her but watched for Remo's reaction. The girl pirouetted and disappeared behind a curtain. The band began to play again, very loudly, and couples returned to the dimly lit floor.

"Let's go," said Remo.

"Are you sleepy?"

"No, but I don't like the way they're playing."

"How do you like the place in general?"

"Wonderful."

"Then let's go."

The contessa crushed her cigarette butt in the ash tray and got up, still staring at Remo. Remo helped her on with her coat, and together they went up the stairs leading to the street. The air that struck our faces was cool and fragrant with the odor of new green leaves. My eyes were reddened by smoke, and I breathed deeply, with a feeling of liberation. I got into the car, shut the door and found myself beside Remo's overheated body.

Only when I got to bed did I realize that I was aching all over. I had an iron band around my head, a sore throat, blistered feet and a bitter taste in my mouth. I fell asleep early in the morning, to the twittering of the birds.

30

I woke up with a sensation of falling. When I opened my eyes it was as if I had floated up from the bottom of the sea.

"Who's there?" I asked sleepily.

"You're wanted on the telephone," Francesco called from the hall.

I slipped on my wrapper and stumbled down the stairs. I was sure it was Cesare. Perhaps it's all off for today, I was thinking. Hesitatingly I lifted the receiver.

"Is that you, Enrica?"

It was Carlo, and I sighed with relief.

"What is it?" I asked feebly.

"Where were you last night? I called and called you."

"I went out for dinner and dancing."

"What time did you get home?"

"Somewhere around three."

"Did you have fun?"

"Yes, I did."

"Do you remember your promise?"

"Yes, I do."

"When can we get together?"

"Today I'm busy."

"Why?"

"I have things to do."

"Cesare?"

"Yes."

"But I can't wait. After all, you promised. You can see him some other time, whenever you want to. But please, to-day . . ."

"Cesare's the one I shan't be seeing again. In a few days he's getting married."

"Call him up. Tell him you have something urgent to do. I simply have to see you."

"No, it can't be done."

"Please, Enrica."

There was a pause. I heard him breathing heavily at the other end of the wire, but I had nothing more to say. Gently I put down the receiver, and we were cut off. I went out into the garden and sat under the magnolia tree. I was quite sure that Carlo would call again. Sure enough, I heard Francesco shouting to me.

"When will you be seeing him?" Carlo asked.

"At four o'clock."

"I'll come get you after that. Say at six. Two hours ought to be enough."

His voice was tense and harsh.

"I don't feel like it, Carlo. I don't want to see you, really."

"But you promised."

"I know. But I couldn't have imagined that I'd have to choose between the two of you."

"You don't have to choose. You can see him first and me afterwards."

"I don't like the idea."

"But you'll have to keep your promise to me."

"Sorry, I can't do it."

"Fraidy-cat!" he shouted, and cut the connection.

I went back to my room, took off my wrapper and tiptoed into the bathroom, where I turned on the hot water tap of the shower. By the time I was dressed lunch was ready. I went downstairs and sat in my usual chair at the dining room table.

"Am I to be all alone?" I asked Francesco.

"They're still asleep," he said, pointing to the stairs. "Up there hugging and kissing until all hours, no doubt. Ugh! So now they have to sleep it off. There's no telling when they'll be up, but they expect me to wait around all afternoon to serve them. It may be four o'clock before they have lunch, and Germana's supposed to be on call in the kitchen as well."

"We came in very late last night," I said lamely.

"What difference does that make? Frankly, they're disgusting. I can't bear to see that young lout lording it over the house and asking for anything that takes his fancy. I'd like to give him a good whipping, I tell you."

He bit his lips in anger as he served me from the silver platter, decorated with a coat of arms in relief. I remembered how I had met him coming out of Pina's room, smoothing his hair. There was just as great a difference of ages between him and Pina as between the contessa and Remo.

"How old is Pina?" I asked with an ingenuous air.

"Twenty-two," he answered.

"She's older than I am."

"For a man it's another matter," he said, in quite a different tone of voice. "Women of a certain age ought to give up that sort of thing if they don't want to make fools of themselves."

Perhaps he guessed at what I was thinking, because he added:

"I'm a special case, myself. I'm just like a boy. You ought to see me. I wear the women out. I can never get too much of it. I can make love twice a day without any effort. Do you know what that means? But it isn't a matter of sentiment. What disgusts me is to see the state this woman has got herself into. As for me, I make a point of never falling in love. Nothing like that for me."

He had come up behind me and was leaning his cheek on

[193]

my hair. Suddenly he kissed my ear. I jumped up out of my chair.

"I understand women," he said, coming after me. "For instance, I know that you're sexy. If I insisted, you'd go to bed with me. But I'm not insisting. No woman that hasn't got a man can hold out for very long. In this house I fill the needs of both Germana and Pina. But they aren't enough for me. If the contessa weren't so old I could have had her any day. I've been here alone with her any number of times, especially just after her husband left her. She used to pace up and down the room, ready to give herself to the first comer. But she's not my type, with that pale face, those glasses and all that powder. She couldn't hope to do any better than that little pansy, who thinks she's a gold mine and is exploiting her to the limit. No, I don't care for her. I like you, though. You're young, with a fresh skin and that long, soft hair with the bedroom smell."

He came up to me again and stretched out his hand to touch my hair. Then abruptly he withdrew it.

"I'm the one that won't touch you," he said. "Get that into your head. It's no use your trying to lead me on. You're a minor, and I don't want to get into trouble."

He laughed and went away. I sat down in front of the fireplace and poured myself some brandy. As I was putting the cork back in the bottle I caught sight of myself in the mirror. I was holding the bottle in one hand and leaning my head slightly over. The gesture and the position were exactly like those of Contessa Bardengo. I stopped short, then as soon as I had put down the bottle I went up to my room. I was bent on getting out of this house as soon as humanly possible.

31

The curve of his cheek, the shadow of his unshaven beard, the blond hair on his neck, the scar behind one ear . . . When my eye reached his armpit I raised it and began all over. The curve of the cheek, the shadow of the beard, the hair on the neck, the red scar behind the ear, the way the arm was joined to the shoulder . . .

I was watching him out of one eye only, because the other was buried in the pillow. Cesare was sleeping, as usual, with his mouth half open and his hair over his forehead. For the nth time I looked at the curve of his cheek, the flat, transparent ear, the scar, which was like a line drawn by a red pencil, the hollow of his eyes, the lowered eyelids with the blond eyelashes, the line of his shoulder and the way it was joined to his arm.

I raised my hand and gently touched his cheek, feeling the roughness of his beard under my fingers. I ran a finger over his ear, explored the curve of his neck and the line of his shoulder. I shivered, because the blanket had fallen off the bed and I was beginning to get goose flesh. Cesare turned slowly around and opened his eyes.

"What's the matter?" he asked.

"Nothing. I was just looking at you."

"Are you sad?"

"A little bit."

"Do you know what I was thinking? When I get back from my honeymoon and settled in the new house, perhaps we can see one another. I don't like the idea of giving you up."

"No."

"Why not?"

"Because I'm sick of living this way. After you're married I want to start a new life."

He started to answer but I shut his mouth with a kiss. He drew back, put his arm around my waist and smiled in surprise.

"How do you intend to proceed?" he asked.

"I don't know. First, I'll look for another job."

"What about Contessa Bardengo?"

"She doesn't need a secretary."

"I didn't think it would last for long. She's too crazy, and you have too little ambition. . . . But I do want to see you again."

"Nothing doing."

"You're a funny girl. If you love me you should want to go on. . . ."

"I won't love you forever."

He laughed and pulled me toward him, almost as passionately as if it were the first time. His attention was concentrated on me, not on Nini and his wedding day.

"But if I beg you to meet me?"

"I won't come."

Cesare frowned. He took my head in his hands and looked into my eyes.

"Do you mean it?"

"Yes, I do."

"You know perfectly well that I care for you, and you shouldn't treat me this way. It's an act of retaliation."

"It isn't retaliation. I simply want someone who's all mine."

"But I'll still be all yours."

"And Nini?"

"Oh, you needn't worry about *her!*"

"Then why are you marrying her?"

"Do you really want to know?" he asked, raising himself on one elbow. "I'll tell you. This is the first time I've admitted it, even to myself. The truth is that I'm fed up with studying, that I know I'll never get a degree. I want a house and a life of my own. I realize I'm not being very fair to Nini. But that doesn't matter. She's been in love with me for years, and I'm making her happy, not doing her wrong. I want a place where I can entertain my friends, a place that's mine, not my father's. And I want to have a job that doesn't call for a degree. Nini's father has a soap factory, I told you that. And I'll be working for him. The lack of a degree won't matter. No one will think of asking about it. Do you understand?"

I nodded. Cesare looked at me sadly. He shook his head and covered his face with his hands.

"I'm an egotist, I know. And to think that only a few years ago I had all sorts of plans and ambitions for the future! I wanted to be an engineer and a builder. But Nini's to blame, too. She's been after me to marry her. She's harped on the fact that I don't need a degree to work in her father's plant. He does everything she wants, and besides he's getting on in years and wants to retire, the old fool. So it's his fault, or rather hers. The good fairy with the blue eyes . . . What makes you laugh?"

He took hold of my shoulders and forced me under him.

"You'll always be mine, even if you don't want to."

"Are you so sure?"

He did not answer, but kissed me savagely and bore down on me so hard that I could barely breathe. His skin had a bitter, salty smell.

"Your father's here," I said, suddenly stiffening.

He sealed my lips with a kiss. His face was so near that I could barely make out its traits—the fleshy, white nose, the full lips, the two horizontal creases in the forehead. Then I saw nothing at all, because his face was glued to mine, his nose on my cheek and his lips on my chin, in total abandon. We lay for a long time like this, in one another's arms, until the telephone aroused us. Cesare reached over me for the receiver, and I felt the cord unwind on my back.

"Yes, don't worry," he said into the mouthpiece, making his voice as agreeable as he could. "I will, I promise. I'll go to the registry office, if necessary. But it's closed now, and I'll have to go tomorrow morning."

He grunted as he replaced the receiver, and then let his hand fall caressingly on my shoulder.

"I must be going," I said.

"Don't go."

"But you have to study."

"Study!" he exclaimed, with an outburst of laughter. "Silly girl! I won't open those books again as long as I live. My father can kick all he wants, but I don't care. I'll slam the door in his face and go to my own house, where I can do what I please. At last I'm free!"

I got up and searched for my stockings on the floor. Cesare got up too. Standing in front of the mirror he watched me out of half-closed eyes.

"I've put on weight, don't you think so?" he said.

"You look exactly the same to me."

"No. Look here. You haven't been watching me very closely. Just see these folds, they weren't there before. I'm getting old, I tell you."

I laughed. To me his body seemed as smooth and slender as that of a young boy. Suddenly something about the photographs of Holland behind me rubbed me the wrong way. One of them was crooked and I put out my hand to straighten it.

"What are you looking at? Those pictures? What's their charm?"

[198]

"I'd like to be in Holland."

"Why Holland?"

"Because almost any place seems better than here."

"Holland's not so wonderful. It's all flat and monotonous. It's always cold, even in summer, and two days out of three it rains. Of course, I went there with big ideas of finding hundreds of blond girls who would be dying to go to bed with me. What a fool I was! I couldn't stand either the climate or the food. I found a girl, but she wasn't much for looks, and I couldn't get rid of her."

He yawned as he pulled on his socks. He paused to listen to a sound on the other side of the door, then went on dressing and at the same time telling me about Holland. Then he took me to the front door and gave me the usual hurried farewell kiss.

"Hold me tight," I said. "This is the last time." I felt my legs giving way beneath me.

"Of course it isn't. We'll be seeing each other."

He insisted on bluffing to the very end. I let myself be pushed through the door and, as usual, I heard the lock spring behind me.

32

At the bus stop I suddenly felt someone grab my arm and turning around saw that it was Carlo.

"I was waiting for you," he explained.

"You shouldn't have done that."

"When I think what Cesare's been doing with you, that he's touched you with his . . ."

"Shut up, will you."

"Now you've got to come with me. I'm not letting you go without one last . . ."

"I'm not having any," I said, freeing myself from his grasp.

He stuck his hand in his pocket and looked at me with a mixture of tenderness and resentment.

"Forgive me," he said. "I've no claim, I know. But I've been waiting and waiting for this afternoon to come, even although I knew you were starting it with somebody else. I've been imagining you and him the whole time, in his bed . . . your body and his body, your legs and his legs, your hands and faces . . . I tried to control my imagination, but I couldn't . . . Here I was, waiting. . . . I've never spent worse hours in my life. Now, you *will* come with me, won't you? I don't care if he's dirtied you, if he's filled you with his smell."

"I'm tired. All I want to do is sleep."

"You can sleep afterwards. I've got to have you."

As he spoke he pulled me toward the far end of the street. With a feeling of unspeakable weariness I followed. We went, silently, in the direction of his house. Once inside he pushed me into the elevator, a hermetically closed metal box, smelling of stale tobacco. He had trouble opening the front door; the key turned idly in the lock until he remembered that the lock was a new one and he was carrying a new key at the bottom of his pocket. As soon as we entered the apartment he locked and bolted the door behind him and pulled me down the long hall leading to his bedroom. The room was bright and cheerful, with white walls, two bookcases, a cot on one side and an improvised wardrobe, consisting of a metal bar with curtains in front of it.

"I like it here," I admitted.

He locked the door and took off his jacket. There were semicircles of perspiration under his arms.

"You've been perspiring," I remarked.

He lifted his hands to his armpits and grimaced.

"It was that long wait," he said.

I took off my coat and sat down on the foot of the bed.

"Now that you're here I feel empty and impotent. I'm not even sure I want you any more."

"I'll put my coat back on, then."

"Wait a minute."

He sat down beside me with his hands on his knees.

"Is this building new?" I asked him.

"Not very."

"How long have you lived here?"

"Six years. Why do you ask?"

"For no special reason."

Suddenly he took his head in his hands and burst out laughing. Looking at him in bewilderment, I saw that tears were rolling down between his fingers.

"What is it?" I asked.

He made no reply, but grasped my neck and pushed me backwards. His fingers dug into my flesh, but I felt curiosity rather than pain. I thought of my mother's body, lying motionless on the bed, and imagined that she must have had somewhat the same feeling when she fainted away. When I gasped for breath Carlo lessened the pressure and, apologetically kissed my mouth and eyes. He loosened his tie and threw it onto the floor, pulled off my sweater and fumbled at the zipper of my skirt. Gently I pushed his hand away and opened it myself. He kissed the places on my neck where he had left the trace of his fingers. "*His* smell is there," he murmured, running his lips over my body and pulling off my slip and brassière. "These are traces of *his* sperm. . . . Here is a bruise which *he* inflicted on you. . . . Here are the marks of *his* teeth. . . ." He buried his head between my breasts, raising it to evoke Cesare's name, and then kissing me again, wildly.

"Shut up!" I shouted.

Carlo stopped short and looked at me seriously, as if he were waiting for me to say something.

"I disgust you, is that it? Go ahead and say so!"

I turned toward the wall.

"Forgive me," Carlo whispered into my ear, rubbing my back with one hand.

"Let go," I said. "I don't want you."

He got up and pulled on his trousers. When I turned to look at him he was white as a sheet. While I was getting dressed I felt the piercing stare of his eyes. He escorted me to the door and held out his hand. I shook it and started down the stairs. Halfway down he overtook me, in his stockinged feet and with his hair in disarray.

"Don't go," he said imploringly. "Come back, won't you?"

I went on down.

"Please."

"No, I can't."

"I'll do whatever you say. I won't force you to make love. I'll talk to you, that's all. I have so much to say."

I was still shaking my head stubbornly as I came to the foot of the stairs. Before going through the door I turned around and saw him sitting halfway up the stairs with his head between his hands.

"Good-bye," I called back, but he did not raise his head or reply.

Outside there was a gentle, tepid rain. Summer is just around the corner, I said to myself, and I'll start a new life. Meanwhile I must go back to the villa. The next day, I promised myself, I would get up early and go look for another job.